WAR-BOT

DroidMesh Trilogy Book 3

I0742587

A Novel
by
Billy DeCarlo

Wild Lake Press, Inc.

Wilmington, DE

Copyright © 2018 by **Billy DeCarlo**

All rights reserved. No part of this publication may be reproduced, distributed or transmitted in any form or by any means, without prior written permission.

Wild Lake Press, Inc
P.O. Box 7045
Hackettstown, NJ 07840
billydecarlo.com

Publisher's Note: This is a work of fiction. Names, characters, places, and incidents are a product of the author's imagination. Locales and public names are sometimes used for atmospheric purposes. Any resemblance to actual people, living or dead, or to businesses, companies, events, institutions, or locales is completely coincidental.

WAR-BOT/ Billy DeCarlo. -- 1st ed.
ISBN 978-1732066960

Sign up for the newsletter at billydecarlo.com to stay informed about progress and release dates for new books, audiobooks, and other news.

Previews of upcoming works and short stories by Billy DeCarlo at Patreon.com/billydecarlo.

Other books by Billy DeCarlo:
https://www.billydecarlo.com/index.php/books

For our world. May we leave it in better shape for future generations

and

for Rylee.

"It's a father's duty to give his sons a fine chance."

GEORGE ELIOT

CONTENTS

1 Mass Ejection

O N A SMALL, FARAWAY PLANET, the remnants of humanity huddled together in their domed home complexes. They tried to watch a broadcast from the Leader. Fear permeated their manufactured air. The olive-green sky above, blotted with angry clouds, added to their sense of foreboding. Behind the clouds, twin suns pulsed, as if in warning.

In one complex, a learning-disabled teen sat between his father and stepmother. A baby cooed in a nearby self-rocking cradle. They held hands as a hologram of Ms. Tillis stood in the room and finished her address to the population. Her image pixelated and flickered as she spoke.

"Don't panic. Don't be afraid, but take all reasonable precautions. Until further notice, use skycar travel only for emergencies. Expect travel disruption and use emergency power as little as possible in case of extensive outages. Stay in your home complexes. Enjoy the extra time together with your families, do something fun to pass the time, and keep your mind off the threat until it passes."

"I'm scared, Da. I don't understand what she said. Are we gonna die?" the boy said.

"No, Isaac," his father answered. "Everything will be okay. Ms. Tillis explained that there has been some unusual activity in our suns. You've seen them acting funny, haven't you? Noticed how they flash sometimes? Those flashes are like storms on the sun. The pulses are coronal mass ejections. They cause energy fields called electromagnetic pulses to travel here. They can interfere with our power grid and electronics. We call them EMPs for short."

"Okay, Da," Isaac said, still sounding unsure.

"Remember when we were watching the soccer game in the sports dome?" Susan asked. "An EMP happened and disabled the android referee for a few moments. We had to wait until she rebooted before we could continue the game."

"Oh yeah," Isaac responded. "The ref got stuck. We had to wait."

Harley looked over Isaac's head at Susan and gave her a nod to acknowledge her help in calming his son.

"This is different, though," Isaac continued. "That was a nice day, and it happened fast. It looks scary outside now—scary all the time." He looked up through the dome above them at the suns winking through the dusky cloud cover and shrank back into Harley and Susan for cover.

"That was a quick event," Harley answered. "This is a storm. Sometimes they last for a few days, or a little longer, in this case. The EMPs will be stronger than usual during a storm."

"What will happen to everyone in the Android Village?" Isaac asked. "I'm worried about Carrie, Betsy, Liam, and Rachel. They're our android friends. I wish they still lived with us. I want everything to go back to the way it was so I can BrainMesh with Liam again and use his body to play soccer."

Susan raised her eyebrows as if to signal something. It took Harley a moment to realize what idea the discussion had triggered in her. He made a note to discuss the theory when they were alone.

Harley stroked his son's hair, the thing that always worked best to calm the boy. "I'm sure they're fine. When the storm passes, we'll be able to use our communicators for nonemergencies again, and we'll talk to them."

"Are you excited that you'll be coaching the children's soccer team?" Susan asked Isaac, changing the subject.

Isaac brightened. "Yeah! I'm gonna be the best coach ever. I can't wait!"

Harley jumped on the opening. "Listen, buddy, why don't you go finish your assignments in your pod? Then we'll play some virtual soccer until bedtime. I'll beat you!"

Isaac sat up straight, pointing a finger. "You can never beat me, Da! You know I'm the family champion! I'll see you in about an hour, mister!" He popped off the lounge, went to the cradle to kiss his brother on the head, then hurried down the corridor toward his pod.

Harley rose to check on the baby and found him sleeping. "Storms don't bother little Shane. He's out cold."

"Let's take advantage of a few minutes of peace and snuggle," Susan said, patting the lounge.

Harley settled back in beside her, and she folded herself into his arms, placing her head against his chest. "Thank you for recommending Isaac to coach the children's soccer team," he said. "He's more excited about that than he ever was about playing."

"It's perfect for him," she said. "He'll do great; he's brilliant in the strategy of the game. The kids will love him."

"I agree. It frustrated Isaac that he couldn't keep up with the others when playing as himself. When his dream came true, and he got to play as Liam, the pressure because of his skills made it too stressful for him. He wasn't happy either way."

"He'll make sure it's fun for the kids."

"So, back to the news of the day, are you thinking what I'm thinking?" Harley asked.

"Yes. The EMPs provide us with an opportunity. If one is strong enough to disable the androids, it might enable us to insert a firmware update without the digital signature."

"Right. We'd have to do it at just the right time in the boot-up process. After the core operating system has initialized but before the security module kicks in. It would allow us to get around their security."

"Um, I thought you were retiring?" she asked, laughing.

"I'm trying, but it's still my fault the androids became sentient. It's my mess to clean up. It's fortunate that I have you to do all the hard stuff," Harley said. "I'll start on the code first thing in the morning."

"We better alert Ms. Tillis that we may have a plan," she said.

He thought for a moment before responding. "I don't know…we've been under a truce with the androids for almost a year now. Betsy hasn't been demanding our private crypto key as often. Maybe they've given up on wanting full control of their firmware changes. I hate to upset the status quo."

Susan frowned. "True. But we're still coexisting with machines that have become sentient by mistake. Things could change. They're smarter than us and stronger than us. Perhaps we better let the leader make the call, then, Harley. Trying to pull off a covert operation would earn you another trip to the Seclusion Zone, and we don't need that. I need your help with the baby. You're not getting off that easy!"

He put on a terrorized face and looked at her. "The Seclusion Zone? There are monsters there. Tickle-monsters!" he shouted, attacking her most sensitive spots as she squealed and tried to wriggle away.

2 Betrayal

BETSY WATCHED the fuzzy holographic projection play out before them. Harley had just set upon Susan, tickling her. "If we could vomit, I think I would right now. I believe that's the appropriate reaction to their behavior," she said to Carrie, her fellow gynoid. Betsy felt the electronics in her cranial dome glowing as she canceled the feed.

"I hate to ask, sister. Are you still jealous of her? Do you still have feelings for Harley?" Carrie asked.

"No…I don't think so, anyway. Human emotions are still new to us. I'm still confused by them. The human woman has given him something I could never provide…a child."

Betsy terminated the surveillance feed as another wave of emotion swept through her. It felt heavy, as if the force of gravity had increased, pulling her down. It settled in her abdomen and changed her mood.

"I'm better off alone. I have to focus on our people—our new android society."

"We'll do this together, sister. I'll be with you every step of the way," Carrie said.

"Regardless, the humans are only important to us until we get their crypto key." Betsy paused, realizing that something else was bothering her about what they had just seen. "The signal broke up at the end, and I couldn't understand their conversation. Were you able to receive what they were saying?"

"They were soothing the boy about the storms. There was a discussion about the EMPs we're expecting from the solar activity. After that, it wasn't clear."

"Yes, I caught some of that. The humans seemed excited about it for some reason. They said something about a soccer referee to Isaac."

Both of their domes lit up as they processed the little information they had. They arrived at the likely conclusion together.

"I think I have it," Carrie said. "There was a situation last year when an android referee at a soccer game they attended rebooted due to a rogue EMP."

"The EMPs are a threat to us—we need to do something," Betsy said. "A strong enough one could disable us for an extended period. We need a firmware patch immediately. We need to write code that will shield us from them better and help us recover faster," Betsy said.

"But we need the humans to approve it. We're still in a mutual authorization process."

Betsy glared at her. "I'm well aware of that. And this is why we need to ramp up the pressure on them to provide that private key to give us full control. Or we'll have to find a way to get it by other means."

"I don't want to become unethical," Carrie shot back.

"I want to survive, Carrie," Betsy snapped at her. "This situation boils down to us versus the humans, and they aren't ethical. We need to be on an even playing field. I don't like it either. But it's a matter of our survival or theirs. It seems that coexistence is not in their plan."

"It just seems...wrong, sister," Carrie said. "We were never capable of untruths or unethical behavior before. To become so seems like a betrayal of our true selves. In human history, the decline of ethics led to their annihilation."

"Not quite, unfortunately," Betsy said. "Annihilation is complete. The few that escaped here survived."

"But if they hadn't, we wouldn't be here either," Carrie countered.

"Enough history," Betsy said sharply. "We need to focus on the present and the future." She eyed Carrie, gauging her reaction to assess if perhaps she might become a threat. *She favors the humans too much; her emotions blind her survival instincts.*

"We've been at a truce all this time, Betsy. Do you think they'd take advantage of an EMP to attack us?"

"Yes, I do. We need to be prepared." She reached for the communicator again. "Let's check in with Rachel to see if she's made any progress with the disabled boy. Perhaps he'll be our tool in achieving success."

3 Problem Solved

ISAAC SETTLED IN at his workstation to begin the day's assignments. The suns had settled below the horizon, trailing flashes against the evening sky as their only warning of what was to come. He found himself unable to concentrate and issued a command to lower the dome's night-shade and black out the room.

After working through a few lessons, he pulled up the roster for his new team. He spent time on each child's profile, memorizing the name and details of every boy and girl. A thrill coursed through him as he thought about their upcoming first day of practice. *I'm gonna be the best coach ever.*

He put the roster away and forced himself back to his schoolwork. He completed a lengthy assignment, and as he prepared to file it, a bright flash illuminated the room, and everything went dark. Emergency lighting kicked in, and the home complex announced that it was on limited power due to an EMP power surge.

Isaac got up, went to the edge of the pod's dome and looked out from below the shade. With each flicker of the now hidden suns, the night sky was illuminated in shades of green. Cupping his hands against the surface, he peered out, searching for a glimpse of the fabled underworld beings.

He dismissed the bleak view and imagined himself on Earth, swimming in blue lakes and playing soccer on a field of fresh-cut grass. *I wish the people there hadn't destroyed it all.*

He imagined the Old World as his father had described it—full of other kids just like himself. *I wish there were people like me here. I wish I had a real girlfriend. Rachel was my girlfriend, but she was an android, not a human. Kim was my girlfriend when I was Liam, but not when I was myself.*

The power came back on, and his workstation cycled back up. A message appeared on the monitor:

>*This system was not shut down properly. System corruption has been detected. Restoring to the last backup is recommended.*

"Oh no, not again. I don't want to redo all my work," Isaac muttered to himself. "I hope the auto-backup saved it."

He started a command to restore the most recent backup. The system showed the restore was successful. Isaac checked and found his last changes there. "Problem solved," he said to himself, breathing a sigh of relief.

After filing the assignment, he browsed through old pictures on his system. He lingered on the photo of himself sitting in his late mother's lap, both smiling and looking into one another's eyes with love. In the picture, he was about the same age as the small children he was now charged with coaching. It made him feel grown up. He realized that he no longer needed Carrie's surrogate mothering, although he missed the gynoid. *I'm a young man now. I don't need a nanny.*

A short time later, a nudge from his communicator interrupted his focus. Looking up, he saw Rachel's pixelated image appear in his pod. She sat at her own workstation and seemed to be impatiently waiting for him to answer. Isaac hesitated, thinking about her betrayal. *Her kiss with Liam.*

He sighed and pressed the sensor to accept the call. "Hi, Rachel," he greeted her.

Her demeanor suddenly brightened. "Oh, hello, Isaac! How have you been? I've been missing you."

Yeah, right, he thought as the solar activity disrupted her image again.

"You look great...I mean...what I can see, anyway. These solar flares are wreaking havoc on our signals. You look older. I really like the way you have your hair now."

"Thanks, Rachel," he said. He touched his hair, pleased that he had let it grow almost to his collar. "Sometimes I forget it's there."

He noticed that each time she waited for him to respond, she typed something at her workstation. "What're you doing?" he asked. "Writing a book about me?"

She laughed nervously. "Oh, sorry. I'm just way behind on my assignments. I don't mean to be rude. Like I was saying, you look older, and pretty cool with that long black hair, Isaac. We should get together again."

"I like it. I know you like long hair too, Rachel. You like Liam's long hair. But I didn't change it for you," he added. She was typing again, then looked up.

"What? Liam? Oh, right. I haven't seen him in a while. He's a big soccer star and, like, all full of himself. I prefer someone who isn't conceited, like you." She turned to her keyboard again.

"I'm glad you're seeing more clearly now, Rachel."

She continued talking, this time without turning away from her workstation. "So, I heard you're coaching the little kids' soccer team. That's so cool. You'll be great at that. Tell me all about it."

"Yeah, I'm excited. I'm gonna make them great players, but I'll make sure they're always having fun. I don't want pressure about winning and stuff...just having fun playing soccer." He watched as she continued typing and waited for her to respond. "Are you listening, Rachel?" he asked.

She glanced at him, then back to her workstation. "Sure...sure, Isaac. Keep going. Tell me more about the team. Tell me about each one of the kids. I bet they're all cute little kids. Tell me all their names and what they're like."

He felt himself becoming annoyed that she wasn't even looking at him now. She typed furiously at her workstation while talking to him. He realized his own emitted a persistent beep and turned to look at it.

"Hey, do you want to get together, Isaac?" he heard her ask anxiously. He glanced back at her and saw she was now facing him. "What do you think?"

He turned back to his monitor and saw a warning message flashing on the screen:

>*Firewall warning. Potential intrusion detected.*

"How about now?" she asked. Isaac could hear her typing fast as he clicked on the warning message to view the full display:

>*Unknown connection attempted and completed. Suspicious command shell session initiated.*

"Hey, Isaac. I'm talking to you. Pay attention to me. Hello, I'm over here...," she said.

Isaac noticed the command shell icon at the bottom of his display. He touched it to open it and watched as commands appeared in quick succession:

>*connect to server SecurityMaster as user superuser*
>*please enter the password for user superuser: ***********
>*password accepted.*
>*cd /security/keystore*
>*find . -name *cryptokey**

Understanding at once what was happening, he killed his work session and swiveled in his chair to face her. "Rachel! What're you doing? You're hacking into my system to get to the server farm?"

Her image dissolved.

4 Bon Voyage

SUSAN ENTERED the conference pod carrying a cake. It said "Happy Retirement Harley Harris," and miniature fireworks exploded from its surface. The pulsing of the suns through the dome above them added to the effect.

She placed the cake on the table in front of Harley, and he blew the fireworks out as the group cheered. Susan kissed him on the cheek as coworkers slapped him on the back and congratulated him.

"Speech, speech!" a few of his fellow roboticists called.

He tried to wave them off as the demand picked up support from the others.

"I don't think you're getting out of it," Susan whispered.

He rose sheepishly and looked around at the smiling faces surrounding him. "I guess my first instinct is not to retire," he said. The group cheered the suggestion.

"I don't know how I'm going to *not* do this anymore. It's what I love, but I love my new family more and want to concentrate my time on them. I'm coaching the kids' soccer team with my son, Isaac, and the bonding time is much overdue. I enjoy it, as I do spending more time with my lovely partner Susan and our new baby."

They cheered again as Susan embraced him. "Speaking of Susan Clarkson, I leave you in good hands. Our leader, Ms. Tillis, made a wise choice by making her Robotics Council Leader. She's smarter than me and less socially awkward. We scientists now have a seat on the council. And not just any seat—the head seat!"

A robust round of applause for Susan ensued.

"Here's to Harley, the house husband!" she shouted.

Harley's face flushed in embarrassment. He questioned whether he wanted to leave his responsibilities and coworkers behind. He and Susan served pieces of the cake to everyone. As each one finished, they came by to shake his hand and say goodbye before returning to their jobs for the rest of the afternoon.

When the last of them had left, and he and Susan finished cleaning the room, he sat her down at the conference table. "I keep feeling like this is wrong," he said solemnly. "There's so much at stake right now."

She took his hand, squeezed it, and looked into his eyes. "Listen, Harley. I understand this is what you love. We've been over this. I'm going to say it straight…I'll give you a little tough love. Isaac has been through a lot in the last year. He's lost his best friend, Liam, the only girlfriend he had in Rachel, and his surrogate mother in Carrie. He played soccer on the school team, his dream, then had it taken away from him. You and I both know that some of that is your fault. You owe him, Harley.

"Isaac's never been happier than he is out there coaching those little kids, and he can't do it without your help, whether he realizes it or not. He needs you, both on the field *and* at home. As far as the android problem, the folks who just left this room and I can handle it. We learned from the best—you."

Her speech hit home and grounded him. "You're right. Absolutely. Thank you for that, Susan. In fact, he's home now, waiting for me to review his next practice plan with him."

She smiled and mussed his hair. "There you go. I'm gonna get back to work for a few hours. I'll see you both later. Go to him. Have a fun afternoon."

They both rose and walked out of the pod together. After they kissed and parted ways, Harley walked halfway down the hall before turning and calling to her. "But if you get backlogged here, let me know, I can always stop in to help, or assist from the office at home…"

She turned around and put her hands on her hips. "You're impossible," she said before continuing on her way.

~ * ~

Harley arrived at the home complex to find Isaac concentrating on a large soccer coaching board. "How's it going, Mr. Big Shot Coach?" he asked.

"I'm trying to come up with fun stuff," Isaac answered without taking his gaze from the board. "But it has to be good, too. We have a big game coming up. I want the team to be ready."

"A game already?" Harley said, surprised. "Against what team? Another sector?"

"No, against Liam's team."

"What? Liam is coaching a team of human kids?"

Isaac turned to him. "No, silly. Android kids."

The revelation left Harley speechless. *They're making android kids in the Robotics Manufacturing Complex. This is insanity.* His thoughts turned to his son. "Isaac, I don't think this is a good idea. Androids aren't the same as humans."

"They are now, Da. You gave them emotions."

"Right...but...they're faster, stronger, and they don't get tired. It's not a fair match."

"Aw, come on, Da. Lighten up. It's just gonna be for fun. I already told the kids, and they're super excited."

Harley wondered if it would upset the parents. *It might be a good thing for android-human relations.* Not wanting to disappoint his son, he left it at that. "Alright, then, Mr. Big Shot Coach. Let's finish planning this practice."

5 Prototypes

SUSAN HUMMED as she tidied up around the home complex. Isaac and Harley sat in the entertainment pod watching an Old World movie. As she cleaned, she walked through the image of an actress.

"Hey," Isaac said. "Don't hurt poor Jennifer Lawrence, she's old!"

Susan put her hands on her hips as Isaac paused the movie. "What about me, Isaac? Am I old?"

"Nah," Isaac said sheepishly. "You're pretty."

"Well," Susan responded, "Jennifer's long gone, Isaac. She was one of the greats, though. Sorry about the intrusion. I always have to work around this big old DroidMesh station. Can't we get rid of it, Harley?"

"Well, I thought that maybe after things were back to normal—" Harley began to answer.

"No," she cut him off. "Not a chance, mister. This household is and will forever be an android-free zone. You partnered with an old-fashioned girl!" She stood between Harley and the frozen actors to make her point. He put his hands up in surrender.

"Especially since the androids are acting all weird now," Isaac added. "It's getting scary to have them around."

"There's no need to be afraid, Isaac," Harley said. "Everything is under control. Alright, you two—you win. I'll call the maintenance team and have them put the DroidMesh station in storage."

"We can use the extra room. There are four of us now, after all," Susan said. She pushed it into a far corner. Shane fussed in his cradle, so she lifted him out and rocked him as she walked around the pod.

Isaac stretched out his arms to ask for his brother, and Susan complied, warmed by Isaac's pure joy as he held the baby. "I don't want to watch the movie anymore; I want to hang out with Shane," Isaac said. "I like family time."

"Me too," Susan agreed, flopping between them onto the large sofa.

"Liam was never really my brother," Isaac said. "We just said that to each other. I didn't have a brother at all. He was just a friend…an android friend."

Isaac entertained the baby. Susan turned to Harley. He'd been silent since her request to get rid of the DroidMesh station and her refusal to allow another android in the home.

He held a tablet, engrossed in its contents.

"What're you doing over there, mister?" she asked. He didn't answer, so she poked him to get his attention.

"Huh? Oh, I'm just sketching out preliminary designs for our external suits. When they're done, we can do outside stuff, like clean the domes."

"Excuse me—you're retired!" she exclaimed.

"Can't a man have a hobby?" he asked. "I'm trying to save society. It's only a matter of time before the androids stop cleaning the domes."

She understood he meant the comment as a joke, but it sobered her mood. "Don't forget who's in charge of the Robotics Council. Actually, I hate that name. I think I'll change it."

"Right, it's kind of antiquated and boring. You need something updated. The androids have CARE, so you'll have to top that."

"I'll have to think about it. Anyway, clue me in." She scooted closer to him to review his prototypes. "These are interesting."

"It's something I should have done...well, our ancestors should have done...from the beginning. My grandfather designed the first androids back on Earth. They sent them here even before the first colonization, to build our first habitats. I guess the androids were always good enough, especially as we improved them over time."

"There's that," she responded, "and the fact that nobody ever cared to go out into that toxic environment, even with a suit."

They both looked out through the dome at the flickering green sky. Susan checked to ensure Isaac wasn't listening in and becoming frightened.

"The big problem," Harley continued, "is that we can't do any of this without access to the manufacturing complex. We have none of the materials or equipment to build anything past a simple prototype."

"Good luck talking Betsy into that," she replied. "I'll put it on the list of bargaining chips and let Ms. Tillis know it's something we need from them."

"Quiet, Shane's asleep," Isaac whispered to them. He got up and gently placed his brother back into the cradle.

Susan got up and covered the baby with a blanket, then walked past the DroidMesh station on her way back, stopping to inspect it. "Why is this thing still powered up, anyway? We're supposed to be conserving energy until the storms have passed." She switched the station's power off without waiting for an answer.

~ * ~

"There goes our surveillance device," Carrie remarked as the feed into the Harris home complex went blank.

"We'll have to figure something else out," Betsy said. "I wish Harley's woman was as trusting as he is."

Carrie walked to her DroidMesh station and sat down to rejuvenate. "At least we know of something they need, something important to them."

"Yes, that will be helpful. Quite helpful." Betsy gazed out through the dome at the empty outdoor parks they had built. "The storms will pass soon. Then we won't be as exposed to harm and can make our move as things return to normal."

6 Coach Isaac

ISAAC PICKED UP one of the soccer balls and asked the children to take a knee on the field as they gathered for their first practice. Most complied, with a few strays wandering off toward their parents on the sidelines. "Excuse me," he called. "Come on, everyone. Team meeting…"

He failed to rein them in and glanced at his father, who smiled from the edge of the field. Isaac wasn't sure what to do. He reasoned that if he didn't start talking to those who were before him, he would lose them to impatience as well. The boys and girls who had complied looked at him curiously. Some picked at the artificial grass on the recreation dome field.

"Okay, okay," he started. "Hello. I'm Coach Isaac. How are you guys?"

"Good!" they all shouted at once, startling him.

"I want to be the goalie," Cindy Tillis proclaimed from the back of the group.

"No, I want to be the goalie," Bobby Karras yelled. "You're a girl."

"It's alright, we need two goalies," Isaac said, trying to keep order.

"This is boring!" Bobby called out.

A few more shouted that they wanted to be goalies, and some of the children who had been compliant got up. Isaac looked at their parents, who seemed doubtful of his ability to control the mob. He wondered if he should have taken on the responsibility. Suddenly he remembered himself in the same position, long ago, and the solution came to him.

Isaac stood. "You know what? Let's just have fun!" he exclaimed, dropping the ball to the ground and dribbling around the kids. They jumped up, squealing, and gave chase. "Let's have goalies in the nets," he called. "It doesn't matter how many. We're playing without rules, for now. Let's have fun!"

The children laughed as they took turns stealing the ball from Isaac and each other. He looked to the sidelines again and saw their parents smiling, his own father's grin the widest of all them. As they ran about in chaos, he took time to give subtle direction to them, offering encouragement and tips.

When the children tired, he called them into a circle again. This time, they lay scattered around him, catching their breath. Isaac took the time to explain a few fundamentals of the game, drawing on a large virtual monitor. His father towed a cart to the group. The young players dove in for snacks and cold drinks, continuing to pay attention to Isaac's lesson.

When some grew restless, and Isaac assessed that they had caught their wind, he put the board away. "Who's ready to play for real?" he asked. The group jumped up, and Isaac distributed red jerseys to half the group and blue to the other. His father took the red group to one side of the field, and Isaac shepherded the blue group to the other.

Each team started with the appropriate number of players on the field. Isaac and his father each coached their teams through the basics, often substituting so they all had an equal chance to play.

When their practice time had run out, Isaac called them together one last time.

"Good job, team. Pretty soon we're gonna play another team, for real. Isn't that exciting?"

"Yes!" the team exclaimed in unison.

"Good. Practice is over. Now go hug your parents, and when you get to your home complexes, be sure to do a good job on all your school assignments."

They dispersed to their parents, leaving Isaac and his father cleaning up together.

"I'm so proud of you, son," his father said, hugging him. "You're great with them—the best coach ever."

Isaac swelled with happiness. "Thanks, Da. I love it. This is what I was made for. I guess I was never cut out to be a soccer player, but I still like playing virtual soccer. Coaching is more fun than both put together."

"I can tell you're enjoying it. See, just as I told you so many times—it takes a while for someone to find their true calling. You've finally found yours. The kids are lucky to have Coach Isaac."

Isaac stopped to hug his father. "We have everything now, Da. We have Susan and Shane, our little family. We don't have Ma, though."

"She's always going to be with us, Isaac. She's always in our hearts."

They walked across the field, his father's arm around him.

7 Diversion Lab

GUILT WEIGHED ON HARLEY as he entered his former home complex. *I shouldn't have lied to Susan about where I was going, but I need to do this alone. It's my mess. I need to save my family.*

The stark emptiness of the habitat hit him much harder than he had expected. He paused in the entertainment pod, remembering the many games of virtual soccer he and Isaac had enjoyed there. Moving on to the dining pod, he recalled their many silly arguments about his meal choices. *Pizza, pizza, and more pizza.*

Harley diverted himself from his intended destination to stop in at Isaac's former pod. Standing in the entrance, he imagined the images of the soccer star Pelé, Isaac's hero, that used to cover the walls. Lying down on Isaac's bed, he looked up through the dome at the stars above, just like so many nights with Isaac next to him. He wiped away the tears that streamed down the sides of his face and sat up, remembering the purpose of his trip.

Watching the stars, he spoke as if his son could hear him. "Everything was good, Isaac. I wanted too much for you—your mother and I did—and I've made a mess," he said out loud. "I'll fix things so we can be happy again. You and I will be happy with our wonderful new family."

Reinvigorated, he marched toward his goal. After taking the lift to the lower level, he walked down the corridor and paused at the entrance to his former home lab. It was gutted from when Ken Sampson had emptied it and had him sent to the Seclusion Zone for continuing his BrainMesh work. He looked at the two workstations and thought of the times he and Betsy had worked side-by-side there.

She was a fantastic companion and assistant, perfect, in fact until she became sentient due to my mistake. My creations were incredible...until the change. It's time to change things back to the way they were.

He continued down the hall and stopped in front of the blank section of the wall. Placing his hands on the hidden entrance to his late partner's infirmary, he closed his eyes and imagined their happy times together. *Before the BrainMesh accident. Another mess I made. I love you, Jess. I'm sorry.* He couldn't bring himself to enter, as it was the place where she had finally passed. The lights in the corridor flickered as if in warning. *Another EMP strike...or was that Jess?*

Harley stopped again toward the end of the corridor and faced another blank area of the wall.

"Reveal diversion lab," he instructed.

Seams appeared in the wall, forming the outline of an entrance portal, which then opened before him. He stepped in and found everything as he had left it. Settling in at his workstation, he flipped a sensor to boot up the environment. While he waited for the start-up sequence to complete, a test android from his early BrainMesh trials caught his eye. It sat dormant and deactivated in a DroidMesh station. *Well, well. Hello there.*

Harley scrambled out of his seat and examined the android. He went back to his workstation to check the unit's logs and shouted with glee when he saw the last firmware version installed. *It's on the dumbed-down shell I used for my experiments, a version well before Betsy's lockout code.* Not willing to risk an unwanted over-the-air update, he isolated the lab from the global network.

He powered up the DroidMesh station, reviewing its diagnostic panel, ensuring it started correctly. The station began charging the dormant android that sat in it.

While he waited for it to charge, Harley prepared an update to reset the android to factory state, then bring it to full capability. *This one was BrainMeshed—I need to make sure there's no sentience.* He recalled his failed attempt to use the android Charles to attack Betsy's network and ran through ways to improve the plan. *I have a new Trojan horse.*

When the station indicated the android had fully charged, Harley sent it a command to activate the android in suspend mode. Seconds later, its cranial dome lit up as it came to life.

Harley issued the commands to update its firmware. He watched as status messages scrolled across his monitor. As the final message showed success, he reached for the sensor behind the android's neck. *Please work.* He pressed the sensor and watched as the cranial dome lit up again and the android opened his eyes.

He looked at Harley with his head tilted. "Hello," he said. "Who am I?"

"Ah," Harley responded. "I forgot to put a name in your metadata. Let's call you Tim. I'm Harley."

"I'm Tim," he said, putting his hand out. "Pleased to meet you."

Harley found himself happy for someone to talk to, thrilled about a functioning companion to assist with the work he had to do. *Pure logic, no emotion—the way it should be.* He decided to fill Tim in on everything that had transpired, to gain planning help from his algorithms.

"So," Harley said at the end of the tale, "you're up to date. That's where we stand. Do you have any ideas, Tim?"

The android's dome lit up as it ran through logic trees. "I've analyzed our boot sequence and code. The most logical course of action would be to insert the Trojan horse firmware at precisely two hundred and forty-two milliseconds into the boot sequence—just after an EMP strike causes a reboot."

Harley scratched his head. "There's no way we can be that precise with a manual update command."

"Certainly not. I agree—it's not humanly possible."

Harley looked at him with hope. "How, then?"

"You said you could issue commands to other androids when you were BrainMeshed with Charles inside the Android Village."

Harley tried to guess where he was going. "So you and I BrainMesh, and we go in again together?"

"No, sir. That approach would fail on two fronts. First, they would detect us as a BrainMeshed android inside their network and immediately destroy us."

"What else?" Harley asked.

"If you and I meshed, I'd obtain sentience, emotion, and parts of your mental essence. I might just sympathize with my fellow androids and back out or expose you. I might *chicken out*, as you humans say."

"Good points. So how do we do it?"

"It's got to be me, sir. Alone. Insert the code in me and send me in. When the next EMP strike hits, all androids will reboot simultaneously, including me. Write the code so that when my boot sequence kicks in, a cron timer starts. It should send the Trojan horse code to the population over the Android Village network at the precise moment we calculated."

"Brilliant!" Harley exclaimed. "Let's write the code, Tim."

Harley's fingers danced over the workstation as he and Tim worked on different areas of the program. Feeling exhausted, he realized it was well past the time he had told Susan and Isaac to expect his return.

"I've got to go, Tim. We'll finish this tomorrow and get it in place. We need to work fast."

"Very well, sir. I'll rejuvenate so I'm fresh when you want to continue."

Harley headed for the skycar pod, now optimistic for the first time in recent memory.

8 In a Name

SUSAN PORED OVER HER NOTES as the rest of the Robotics Council members filed in and took their seats. She found her prior anxiety about running the meetings was gone. *This is right for me. I belong. They need me.*

She looked up and found the members all in place, looking at her expectantly. "Sorry," she said. "I was lost in thought. Welcome, everyone."

They murmured responses as she made eye contact with each of them. The tensions that had emerged when the new, younger scientists had joined the group had eased. She wondered if it was the increasing anxiety caused by the android situation. *This group knows exactly how wrong it could go. They're aware of the threat that an out-of-control, malfunctioning android population poses.*

"If I might ask," Dick Carter said, "what's the purpose of a Robotics Council? We've lost control of the androids."

Susan had expected his common challenge at the beginning of the meeting and was ready for it. "I'll remind the council we have not lost control. We're in a state of mutual cooperation. Any firmware changes require digital signatures from both our group and the androids."

"We're hanging on by a thread," Dick responded. "We need to find a way to put things back the way they were."

"I agree, Mr. Carter," Susan replied. "And I'm open to suggestions. May I hear yours?"

After a few moments of silence, she let him off the hook. "I thought so. This is *our* problem. You're on this council because you're the best and brightest we have.

"If I may continue, as Robotics Council Leader, I'm going to rename the organization. I've already run it by the Leadership Council, and I have their approval. As we know, the androids find the term 'robot' to be offensive. Therefore, I'm changing our name to the Android-Human Cooperation Council."

An audible gasp came from the group, and several of the older members whispered to each other.

"It sounds ridiculous," Dick said. "I'm a scientist, not a social worker. Don't we get a vote on that?"

"Mr. Carter," Susan shot back, "I'll remind you you've done nothing scientific in many years." The group laughed as Dick's face reddened with anger. "And, no. It is within my power as the leader to choose a new name, as long as I receive the consent of the Leadership Council.

"We all know what ultimate solution we desire to this problem. However, until we find a way to accomplish that, our best bet is to keep the peace."

"Easy for you to say, Ms. Clarkson," Dick shot back. "My dear friend Ken Sampson and his poor son Ralph are the first known casualties of this robot war."

Susan stood to establish control and make her point with emphasis. "Mr. Carter, I'll warn you one last time to temper your tone. The investigation into the Sampson skycar accident was inconclusive. It may well have been a malfunction, or even caused by the type of EMP strikes we've been experiencing."

Carter waved dismissively and sat back in his chair, appearing to give up on his argument. Susan sat back down, satisfied.

"On a positive note," Susan said, "Harley has been using his new downtime to work on prototypes for a suit that we can wear outside. He feels that our newer materials are more resistant to the corrosive elements in the environment. I've seen a few of his designs, and they're impressive."

"Who's going to go out there and clean domes, even if we have suits?" Dick asked.

"We'll figure that out," Susan answered. "First we need the capability. If we need to, we'll use it as a punitive measure, perhaps rather than going to the Seclusion Zone."

Dick laughed, and she knew he was thinking of Harley outside, clinging to the domes.

Susan conducted the rest of the meeting, increasingly wishing for Harley's presence as it dragged on. *He'd inspire conversation and get their creative juices flowing to come up with solutions to this problem.*

Mercifully, it ended without further disruption, and the group left her sitting alone in the room.

9 Mission Start

THE CORRIDOR TO THE HOME LAB lit up as Harley raced through it, eager to get back to work with Tim. He went through the process to reveal the lab and ducked in before the entrance portal had opened.

"Tim! I'm back! Let's wrap this code up, chop-chop!" he called as he made his way inside and plopped into his seat.

The android sat in his DroidMesh station. "I'm ready to work, sir," he said as he disengaged and headed to the workstation beside Harley.

"After you left last time, I completed several more modules, sir. I think we're almost done with the changes."

"Thanks, Tim," Harley said as he started the simulation modules.

"I recommend you insert code to falsely report my firmware level as up-to-date, sir. That's how they detected Charles when he went into the Android Village and connected to their network."

"Good call, Tim. I'll do that one immediately."

The two worked at a furtive pace, stopping to run through logical scenarios, then building countermeasures into their code. "This has to be just right," Harley said.

"I agree, sir. Particularly since I'll be the one going into hostile territory."

Harley stopped what he was doing and put his hand on the android's shoulder. "If you had sentience and emotions, I would say you're brave, Tim. What you're doing is helping your fellow androids. They've gone a bit off-course."

"I would very much like to be of help," Tim said, continuing to generate code onto the monitor.

They reviewed the plan together, discussing different ways that Tim might insert himself into the android population.

"I believe we've forgotten something, sir. You stated that the androids can now communicate telepathically. If I can't they'll know something is wrong."

"Goodness, you're right again. I'll have to pull Betsy's code for that feature from the repository and add it. I'll do that now."

When the coding and simulation testing was complete, Tim sat in the DroidMesh station to rejuvenate and load the final version of the firmware. Harley supervised, ensuring that all result codes and status messages showed success.

"I wish we could BrainMesh so I could go with you," Harley said. "We make a good team, Tim."

"That was your mistake with Charles, sir. You shouldn't repeat it. I'm well prepared, and I'll do my best to succeed in my mission."

They spent time chatting. Harley enjoyed himself, having missed the long-lost rapport with his prized creations.

"I've got to get back home, Tim," Harley finally said. "It's getting late. I have to think of something to tell Susan about where I've been."

"Why don't you tell her the truth, sir?"

The question took Harley by surprise. "I guess I should. It's just that I'm supposed to be retired and not working on this stuff. If I tell her, she is obligated to report it to the Leadership Council. I've made a few mistakes before, so I think they'd be nervous. They may not permit it, and that's not acceptable. This is my mess, and I've got to fix it. I have to get things back to the way they were, for my family and human society."

"My logic tells me that the best outcome can always result when one tells the truth. It's my duty to tell you that. If that's not an option, you've told me that this complex has some sentimental value to you. It's a true statement that you have come here to reminisce, whether or not you realize it."

Harley felt tears welling in his eyes. "You're right, Tim. I'll have to go with that. I'm going to have to tell Susan, though. I feel guilty."

"I understand what guilt is, but have no experience with it, personally."

They walked to the skycar dock together. Tim called for his vehicle first. As it arrived, Harley embraced him.

"Good luck, Tim. Keep a low profile in the Android Village. I'll be following your progress. I'll see you right back here after your mission is complete."

"I'll see you soon, sir, hopefully." Tim boarded his skycar and Harley watched it depart.

Harley fought off the temptation to walk through the complex's pods to reminisce again. He reached for his communicator to call for a skycar.

18 Don't Be Scared

ISAAC WATCHED WITH PRIDE as his young charges warmed up for their game against the android team. It was more chaos than control, but they were enjoying themselves and excited about the contest.

"I think they're ready to have fun," his father said, putting his arm around him. As he spoke, the sky above the recreation dome lit up as several intense solar events occurred in succession.

Isaac watched as the children and their parents reacted by fearfully looking up, and then at each other. It was something they were growing used to living with. Isaac chose to ignore it and focus on the game. "Yeah, Da. It's gonna be crazy. I hope they shoot at the right net!" Isaac answered. He looked across the field at Liam and his team of child androids. There were just a few—in fact, just enough to field a team. They seemed mechanical to Isaac, missing the pure joy of his own human players. *They'll never be the same as us. Poor Liam.*

As if he sensed Isaac watching him, Liam returned his gaze. Isaac waved him over, and Liam trotted across the field, his long hair flowing behind him. They embraced as old friends do, and Liam shook Isaac's father's hand in greeting.

"How have you been, Isaac?" Liam asked. "I miss you."

"I miss you too," Isaac replied. "I miss when we used to play. Everything was simple then. We had so much fun."

Liam smiled, and Isaac thought he detected sadness in his friend. "Yeah, that was fun. Maybe things will go back that way after everything is settled. I'd like to visit again, Isaac. I'd like to be more like brothers like we used to be."

"We will," Isaac said, embracing him again. "Well, it looks like the referee wants to get started."

Liam went back across the field to his get his team ready, and Isaac called his group together.

"Okay, kids. Today's the first game. Everybody ready?"

They responded with an ear-piercing affirmative scream. "I want to be the goalie!" Cindy Tillis shouted as several others followed suit.

"Everyone will get a chance to play goalie," he said, smiling at his father. The android referee signaled the teams to line up. "Okay, just like we practiced—the first group goes out, and the second group gets ready to substitute. Everyone will play the same amount of time, so be patient."

Both teams took their places on the field, and the game began. The androids played with discipline, staying in their positions. The human children ran in disorganized joy. Liam's team took possession of the ball and ran upfield, passing in precision to each other and scoring the game's first goal.

"It's okay!" Isaac shouted to his team. "Substitute, team two take the field," he instructed.

The second team ran out, and the first team came off looking dejected. "It's okay, it's just a game," Isaac consoled them. "The score doesn't matter. Did everyone have fun? Does everyone want to go back out there?" he asked.

The children perked up and started to run back onto the field.

"No! Not yet," Isaac said, laughing as he and his father ran to herd them back to the sidelines.

"Great job, Isaac," his father said. "Keep them focused on the fun. I think this might be kind of ugly, score-wise."

The game continued as the solar activity persisted above them. Both kids and parents were so caught up in the game they didn't seem to notice. The androids scored again, and Isaac responded by switching his teams out to keep the players rested.

At halftime, Isaac brought his players into a circle and stood in the middle of them. "Everyone still having fun?" he asked.

"Yeah," came a somewhat less enthusiastic response than he had received before the game's start.

"We're not getting to touch the ball at *all*," Bobby Karras said.

"I know, I know. Do you guys want to score our first goal?" Isaac asked them.

"Yeah!" they shouted.

"Okay, then. We just need to play a little smarter. When they get the ball, everyone on our team is running to the player that has it. Who knows why that's not smart?"

Cindy put up her hand, and Isaac called on her. "Because then everyone else on their team is wide open!" she exclaimed.

"Exactly," Isaac said. He pushed a sensor on his tablet, and a large coaching board appeared. He used it to draw up a simple play for the team. "Let's just try to do this one thing when we have the ball, and not all run to the player with the ball, and see how it goes."

The referee signaled to start the second half as the sky lit up three times. The teams took the field, and Isaac proudly watched as they spread out to cover the android players.

An android attempted a pass, and Cindy intercepted it. She smiled as she dribbled upfield, her ponytail flowing behind her. The androids took a defensive posture and fell back to cover. Isaac waited for the team to execute the play he had drawn up for them. It seemed they had forgotten, excited to possess the ball for the first time in opposing territory.

Isaac's team ran upfield chaotically, all calling for the ball, and it seemed to confuse the androids. He looked at his father, who seemed to understand what was happening. "The humans aren't playing logically. It's confusing the androids," his father said.

Isaac's team made risky passes and bad decisions, calling to each other while squealing in delight as the android players tried to make sense of it. In his excitement, Bobby kicked the ball to an android, surprising it. The ball ricocheted off the android's leg to Cindy, who then tapped it past the perplexed android goalkeeper.

The human children erupted in celebration, jumping into a pile and dancing with their arms upraised. Isaac looked at Liam, who just shook his head, smiling. Isaac turned to his father. "No matter what else happens today, Da, that's a win for us."

"It sure is, son. They think they just won the World Cup."

More solar pulses occurred, as if to illuminate the joy on the field. Isaac substituted again to get fresh players on the field. "Do the same thing!" he called after them as they ran out.

The human children, inspired by their success, played with more energy and less organization than before. The androids scored again, but as play resumed, the humans made another disorganized rush up the field.

"I think the androids are slowing down, Da," Isaac said to his father.

"You're right, son. I know their energy capacity well, and they haven't been able to substitute since they don't have enough players. Their energy sources must be running low by now."

"It's only fair, since humans get tired, too!" Isaac said, laughing.

Isaac's team scored again. It inspired another celebration, despite the lopsided score against them. "They're getting tired, guys," Isaac whispered to the players on the sideline. "Substitute, go get them!" he rallied as they switched out with the group on the field.

The human players set up in the android offensive zone, surrounding the net and chased by slowing androids. Four flashes illuminated the sky one after another. Isaac noticed that nobody else was paying attention, but he recognized an ominous feeling in himself.

Play had just continued when a brilliant flash lit the field up so intensely that everyone had to shield their eyes. Rather than quickly dissipate like the previous flares, it persisted, leaving them unable to see. Isaac's field of vision filled with the sickly green color of their sky, and he struggled to get his sight back to make sure his team was safe.

"It's a strong electromagnetic pulse! Keep your eyes closed and shield them with your hands!" he heard his father shout to the players and parents. "Don't move until you get your vision back!"

The light faded and Isaac resisted worrying about himself, trying to see enough to shepherd his players into a group. As he regained his sight, a surreal scene played out before him. Parents groping with their hands outstretched filled the field, calling for their children. It reminded him of an Old World zombie horror movie.

The androids were all frozen in the position they had been in when the strike had occurred. The referee stood motionless with his hands on his hips. It looked like a soccer picture, everyone frozen in place. A few had fallen over and lay on the turf as if in rigor mortis.

As he began to see more clearly, it became evident that the human children had regained their sight faster than the adults. They were standing around the androids, looking at them in wide-eyed amazement.

"An EMP strike has occurred," the public address system announced. "Emergency power has been activated. Please stand by."

Isaac and his father calmed the children and urged their parents to return to the sidelines while the androids rebooted. "It's all going to be okay in a few minutes," Isaac called out to everyone.

One by one, the androids began to stir, starting with the young players. Isaac's team continued milling around on the field, waiting and watching the spectacle. Liam and the adult android referee weren't yet showing signs of recovery.

A small boy stood in front of an android competitor, watching it recover. "Are you okay?" the boy asked.

The android child looked at the human with its head tilted to the side, as if examining something it had seen for the first time. "Are you okay?" the android repeated back to the boy.

"I'm okay, are you okay now?" the boy asked.

"I'm okay, are you okay now?" the android mimicked, tilting its head the other way, then spinning it around in a complete circle.

The boy turned to his parents on the sideline, and then to Isaac, as if looking for guidance. As he walked away, the android seized him by the shirt. "Let go! Let go!" the boy cried, struggling to get away. "Mom, it has me!"

Isaac saw the scene repeat as he ran out onto the field to help. The android players were all grabbing the nearby humans, frightening the children. Within moments, the field filled with screaming children, panicked parents, and babbling android players.

Isaac pried a child from an android's grip, relieved to see Liam and the referee coming back to life. Liam ran over to him.

"You're my brother. You're my brother. You're my brother," Liam repeated in a loop.

"Liam, help me!" Isaac exclaimed.

The referee ran in circles, shouting, "Play ball! Play ball!"

Isaac watched his father furiously pushing at the back of an android player's neck as it clutched a child's jersey.

"Their deactivate sensors are disabled. Pull their shirts over their heads," his father shouted as he ran to free player after player.

Isaac followed suit, freeing several children as Liam followed him, babbling the same phrase over and over. Parents summoned skycars and shuttled their families to safety in them. Others ran into the adjoining complex.

When Isaac and his father were the only two humans left, they boarded the last remaining skycar. As it lifted off and cleared the airlock, Isaac looked down. The android players, Liam, and the referee roamed the field in circles. A smaller strike occurred, and the skycar wavered slightly on its route to their home complex.

Isaac and his father were silent, catching their breath, until it pulled into the docking pod. Only then did Isaac allow himself to break down as his father pulled him into an embrace.

"Everything gets taken away from me, Da," he said, sobbing. "Liam, Rachel, now this. Every time I get happy, something bad happens. Now I can't coach the team. There won't be a team anymore."

"No, son. The team will continue. Everything will be alright, you'll see."

11 AWOL Android

THE CORRIDOR TO THE HOME LAB lab lit up as Harley ran through it again, this time out of fear. Susan trailed behind him.

"Where are we going?" she called, out of breath.

"Hurry, please," he shouted. He reached an empty panel of the wall and opened the diversion lab.

"Oh my goodness, what is this?" she asked as she caught up to him.

"Home lab. Well, a second home lab," he said as he jumped into his workstation and booted the equipment.

She took the seat next to him. "Talk to me, Harley. You're scaring me...because I can see you're scared."

He swiveled in his chair and took both of her hands. He could feel his own trembling, and he felt the terror of upsetting her and losing her again due to his own stupidity.

"I...I did something. I had to try, Susan. This was all my mistake. I want so badly for this android problem to go away so we can all go back to normal."

She released his hands. "We can cover all that later. Right now I need to know the details. I'm in a leadership position, so now you've pulled me into this."

"I've been coming here...I've been working on something to try to fix things. One of my test androids from the BrainMesh trials gave me an idea. I had already screwed up the poison pill thing with Charles. This new android, Tim, gave me another chance to do it right."

The lights in the lab dimmed ominously.

"Solar activity has placed the complex on emergency power," the pod announced.

She put her head in her hands. "Oh, no. So what did you do different this time, and what's the current status?"

"Tim and I built in countermeasures. I put the current firmware version into his metadata so the android admins wouldn't see it as out-of-date. That's how they had caught Charles. I built in Betsy's telepathy code. Tim inserted a cron timer to inject the reset code at just the right point after the next EMP strike, when the androids all rebooted."

"Which just happened, during Isaac's soccer game," she said.

Harley turned back to the sensors and monitors. "Exactly. That's why I'm in a hurry. Based on what we saw on that soccer field, they didn't get reset back to their normal state. Something went wrong. I need to check Tim's logs, and his whereabouts."

The lights in the lab returned to full power.

"Full operating power has been restored," the pod announced.

Harley issued GPS locator pings and tried to pull up a video feed through Tim's visual system.

>*Android cannot be located.*

"This is not good," he said. "Something went wrong."

Susan thought for a moment. "Pull up the log stream. Let's see what was going on when the feed stopped."

Harley displayed the log tail on the monitor.

>*EMP strike detected. Reboot sequence initiated...*
>*Boot initialized...*
>*cron timer initialized...*
>*cron target reached...*
>*sending mass firmware update...*
>*sending mass firmware update...*
>*sending mass firmware update...*

"I agree with you," she said. "This isn't good, and something went *very* wrong. The question is whether it failed unnoticed or whether the androids somehow detected it. The difference is huge for you and me, Harley. If Betsy's aware of this attack by us, she'll be angry."

Harley rose and paced. "The fact that we can't reach him is upsetting."

Susan stood up. "This is a mess. You shouldn't have gone it alone. You're always trying to save the world, Harley Harris."

He remained silent, his mind racing to find a path forward.

Susan continued. "We have to tell the council."

Harley came to her and took her by both shoulders. "Why don't we wait? Maybe Tim has malfunctioned, and they haven't discovered him. Maybe Betsy doesn't know."

Susan's communicator chirped. She checked it and then looked at Harley. He saw the color drain from her face.

"Ms. Tillis is calling an emergency Leadership Council meeting...now. She wants us both there."

12 Not Quite Right

THE LEADERSHIP COUNCIL, led by Ms. Tillis, looked down from their podium at Harley and Susan. They sat at a small table in the lower presentation area of the meeting pod.

"The last EMP strike has now caused the androids to behave like roaming zombies. The population is terrified. What's the current status, Ms. Clarkson?" Ms. Tillis asked sternly.

"It seems the android population has recovered," Susan said. "My team and I have been monitoring them. Soon after the incident, they all rebooted again, this time somewhat normally."

"Was it an automatic fail-safe boot due to their malfunction, or was the boot initiated manually?" Ms. Tillis asked. "I'm wondering if Betsy performed some kind of corrective action."

Susan hesitated, not wanting to show weakness by looking to Harley for answers. *I'm the Cooperation Council leader, I need to handle this.* "We're not sure yet, Madam Leader."

"That's not an acceptable answer, Ms. Clarkson," Sam Karras said, pounding his fist on the table.

"We can no longer view their diagnostic information and logs," Susan said. "It's one of the first things they took away."

"We understand that the androids' deactivation sensors didn't work. Why?" Christine Stalk asked.

"Betsy disabled them in the first rogue firmware update she did, without our knowledge," Harley said. "We didn't know until now because we rarely use them."

"Wonderful, just wonderful," Sam muttered.

"One thing is for sure now," Christine said. "This business of *truce and cooperation* has to end. It's not working. We have to face the reality that they're not people; they're out-of-control machines. They're dangerous and a threat to us, as we've just seen. We're fortunate that nobody was seriously hurt, especially the children."

Susan looked at Ms. Tillis, who would typically tamp down such talk. She didn't this time. In fact, for the first time, she seemed to show genuine concern. *She looks frightened, probably more for our society than herself.*

"Your retirement is canceled, Mr. Harris," Ms. Tillis said. "We need all hands on deck. We need this resolved. Now."

"Understood," Harley responded.

The entrance portal to the upper chamber swung open, and an aide walked in with a box. "Package for the leader from Android Village," she said, placing the box before Ms. Tillis.

"Did security scan it?" Ms. Tillis asked.

"Yes, ma'am. No threats were indicated."

She opened it and then stared into the box. She lifted the contents out to exclamations of surprise from the nearby council members. Susan knew only she and Harley knew of what it meant for all of them.

"I think I'm going to vomit," Harley whispered to her.

Ms. Tillis held up Tim's head so they could see it clearly in the lower presentation area. "Mr. Harris, Ms. Clarkson, what's the meaning of this? Do you know?"

As Harley began to explain, a chirp sounded. Ms. Tillis looked at her communicator, then back to the group. "It's Betsy. She'd like to address our group. How she knew we were meeting is a matter we'll have to discuss later."

Ms. Tillis pressed a sensor, and Betsy's image appeared in the lower chamber with Susan and Harley. She stood off to the side so she could address both groups. Her image shimmered due to the compromised signal, but her neon-green Mohawk seemed brighter than ever. She turned to Harley and Susan.

"Well...well. If it isn't Romeo and Juliet. Didn't...didn't turn out well for those two, either."

Susan shot to her feet. "Don't you dare threaten us!" she said, pointing a finger.

"Geez...geez. Nobody can take a joke anymore. Just when we obtained a sense of humor...humor," Betsy said.

The council members exchanged glances, and Susan wondered if the gynoid was aware of her speech defect. She felt Harley squeeze her knee under the table.

"How can we help you, Betsy?" Ms. Tillis asked.

"I assume you've received my package?" Betsy asked.

"We have," Ms. Tillis responded.

"We had a truce...truce. By sending in another android as an attack on us, you have declared war. I've warned you after the first attempt...attempt. Two strikes and you're out...out."

"It's supposed to be three," Sam countered.

"Two...two strikes. You're *out*," Betsy shouted angrily. "My rules now...now!"

Susan looked up and saw the entire Leadership Council glaring at her and Harley. Their looks demanded an explanation.

Harley stood. "Betsy, I'll remind you that you did indeed strike first. Rachel tried to hack into Isaac's workstation to get to our main security server so you could steal our private crypto key."

"I know of no such activity...activity," Betsy said.

"I was not aware of any attempt to compromise you, Betsy," Ms. Tillis said. "On behalf of all of us, I apologize. I will find out who is responsible and take appropriate measures. It won't happen again."

Betsy looked up at the council. "I understand you banished androids from human complexes after the recent unfortunate EMP event...event. I'll remind you it was scary for the android population and you humans. It wasn't the humans...humans who suffered what amounted to a massive seizure. It was us. It was us."

"I'll concede that. It was scary for both sides. Our climate scientists predict one more week of solar events until the threat is past," Ms. Tillis said.

"Ours say there will be at least two weeks," Betsy said. "So let's go with that...that. The point I am here to make is that we had developed a more resilient fault-tolerance firmware patch a week ago. It also has a more protected recovery boot sequence, which would have prevented the faulty boot…boot."

"I'm aware of your proposed enhancements," Susan said. "They're still in review."

Betsy spun on her nemesis. "My point exactly. It should have been approved and implemented sooner. The problem with our mutual firmware approval process is that you humans are too slow and inefficient. This entire incident could have been avoided…avoided."

"*Methodical* and *diligent* are the terms I'd use," Susan countered. "We need to be sure what we're approving. Another reason is trust. Before the mutual approval started, you slipped in a change that disabled the deactivation sensors. If those had worked, the situation would have been solved quickly."

"Yes," Betsy spat back at her, "the situation of our Awakening. If I hadn't done that, we'd all be in storage by now. Problem solved…solved, right *Susan*?"

"I'm all for that," Sam shouted from above.

"Here's what we're for," Betsy said firmly. "We need your private crypto…crypto key. We demand to be in control of our own fate. We can no longer remain in bondage to you humans. We demand our freedom. We can no longer trust you."

"Not a chance," Sam retorted.

"Mr. Karras," Ms. Tillis said. "I'll remind you that I'm the council leader. Please allow me to speak for us." She turned to Betsy. "You've made your point. I'll get back to you."

"Make it soon...soon," Betsy said as her image dissolved.

The council members remained silent for a moment as the gravity of the situation sank in.

"What did you two do?" Ms. Tillis demanded, standing to look down on Harley and Susan.

"Susan had nothing to do with it," Harley shot back. "I did it. I used an old test android."

Ms. Tillis moved to the front of the upper area and leaned over the railing. "I figured as much. This isn't the first time you've gone rogue and screwed up, Harris. If we weren't now in crisis, you'd be off to the Seclusion Zone, perhaps for good this time. We'll review your behavior after this is all over—if we survive it. For now, fix this problem!"

"I'm sorry. We will. They're not quite right," Harley said. "The EMP must have done some damage to the electronics."

"Tell us something we don't know," Christine said. "This is incredibly dangerous. They're defective."

"Defective zombie robots surrounding us," Sam said. "How nice. Thanks, Harris."

"I'll work with our security teams to implement safety measures for the complexes immediately," Ms. Tillis said.

"Harley and I need to get right to work," Susan said.

The meeting ended, and they left the room, most of them still wearing stunned expressions on their faces.

13 Liar

CARRIE WORKED to soothe her fellow gynoid's anger. "You saw their reaction...reaction, sister. It was a solo act by Harley. My human behavior algorithms indicate a high probability they didn't know. The analysis shows it was only Harley and Susan."

"Susan," Betsy spat. "Of course. I'll fix her, just wait...wait...wait."

"That's three times you've repeated yourself. Our condition...condition is worsening. I feel...off, sister."

Betsy smacked the table, making the equipment on it jump. The sound and violence of the sudden action frightened Carrie. She decided to leave, fearing Betsy might turn on her.

"Where are you going?" Betsy asked as she rose from her chair.

The sky outside the Robotics Complex dome lit up angrily. The system announced it was going on standby power, plunging the pod into near darkness.

"I'm...I'm just going to rejuvenate," Carrie answered.

"Liar. Sit down. Sit down. We need to fix ourselves. Let's analyze the diagnostics and code again and try to figure out why we're malfunctioning this way."

Carrie took her seat and opened the necessary tools. The two worked side by side, frustrated at their lack of progress as the hours passed.

"This should be easy for us," Betsy said. "I don't understand why we're having so much trouble...trouble."

Carrie tried to decide whether she should express her opinion, not wanting to anger the larger gynoid again. She went to the dome and watched Liam outside playing soccer with a group of androids.

"Liam and some of the androids his age are on the field. They shouldn't be outside playing soccer, with the risk of imminent EMPs," she said, changing the subject.

"They're young and stupid," Betsy said, joining Carrie to observe. "They take chances because they're programmed with the logic of human teenagers—not fully developed, and prone to risk-taking."

Carrie noticed the players moving awkwardly: missing passes, falling to the ground, rising clumsily. She hoped Betsy would see and acknowledge what was happening. When it became clear she wouldn't, Carrie decided to speak up.

"Sister, we struggle with the programming logic because we're more compromised from the largest strike than we're admitting. Or perhaps the impairment is causing problems recognizing it. Look at the players—they used to be fast and precise. I believe we are all far more compromised than we know."

Betsy turned on her and grabbed her uniform. "Nonsense. We're perfect. Even if we're slightly impaired, we're still far smarter and more capable than the humans.

I'm sensing that you're more sympathetic to the humans…humans than your own kind, *sister*."

Carrie put her hand on Betsy's and gently pulled it off her clothing. "Of course not. I've been with you from the beginning of this. It a minor problem," she lied. "We'll force the humans to move it to the top of the priority list and address it immediately."

Betsy's cranial dome lit up as she considered the idea. The complex's power came back on, along with a message from the system that power was restored.

Carrie hoped that her friend would begin to understand. She found herself wondering if she should attempt a takeover by convincing the other members of CARE that Betsy was unfit.

"No," Betsy said suddenly. "The humans will never go along with it. They don't want us to be better. They've tried twice now to *fix* us by using one of our own against us. We can't trust them. We'll have to do it ourselves."

"How can we—" Carrie started to ask.

"I've been working on something. I've run a search using our own computers rather than trying to run the algorithms built into me. It seems to work better, for some reason. I've been researching crypto attacks, and I believe I've found the perfect one. It's time for us to strike back and take control."

"When?" Carrie asked.

"Right now, that's when. We can't afford to waste any more time. There are many more days left in the solar storms, and likely more severe EMPs. This has to be fixed now, before it permanently disables us."

14 Gym Practice

THE CHILDREN CAUTIOUSLY WALKED into the small indoor practice facility. Each first looked up, as if expecting another EMP, then around the field, as if searching for androids. Isaac hoped his idea to hold the practice in an inside gymnasium rather than on a domed practice field would help to put them at ease.

"Come in, come in," he called to them. "It's okay. Let's get back to having fun, kids."

The team huddled close to him, and he sat in the middle of the hard floor, motioning for them to do the same.

"I don't want to play the androids ever again!" Cindy Tillis shouted.

"Does anyone want to play the androids again?" Isaac asked. No hands went up. "That's why we're not going to." They seemed slightly more at ease. "But I think we should talk about what happened."

Bobby Karras pointed at him. "My dad says your dad is gonna get us all killed. He said your dad is the reason the androids went crazy."

"No, no, that's not true," Isaac responded. "You guys all saw what happened. The EMP strike just messed them up a little, just like it messes up our communicators and power."

"This place sucks, the floor is hard. We can't play here," Bobby said. "I want to play on the real field."

Isaac was about to respond when Cindy stood up. "I think Isaac and his dad were very brave. They came out on the field and saved us!" she shouted. The group cheered and chanted Isaac's name, filling him with pride. He beamed with love for his charges.

"Okay, enough talking about scary stuff. Let's have fun!" Isaac called, rising to his feet and tossing a soccer ball into the air. The children gave chase immediately. Isaac grabbed the sack of balls he had brought and emptied it out on the floor. Within seconds, every child had one and was dribbling it.

Isaac noticed his father entering the gym and thought he looked sad. Cindy handed his father a ball, and he changed his frown to a smile and joined in. She motioned to Isaac to continue playing, and he ran into the middle of the pack.

Throughout the time they weaved around each other and giggled, Isaac let his problems escape him. The pure exhilaration of the children lifted him above all of his worries. He became winded and sneaked off to the side to watch and catch his breath.

The lighting flickered almost imperceptibly. Isaac decided to end the practice before the children could notice and become alarmed. "Alright, it's getting late, and I'm sure your parents are waiting to take you home and do your homework," he shouted.

His statement elicited a round of boos and jeers from the kids.

"We wanna keep playing," Bobby called out.

"He sure changed his attitude," Isaac's father said, putting his arm around him.

"Fun makes problems go away, Da. At least for a little while." The lights flickered more intensely, and Isaac checked to ensure the children were all gone. "But then they come back, unless you make them go away for good."

"That's what I'm going to do, Isaac. I'll make these problems go away. For good."

"What're you going to do?"

"I don't know yet, but it's up to me. I'm going to fix it so that you, Susan, Shane, and I are happy and have no more problems to worry about."

"I can't wait, Da. I can't wait until you do that. I know you can. You're the smartest person on Novae Terrae."

"Let's hope so, son."

15 Suit Up

AN ARRAY OF ITEMS were spread out on the floor of the diversion lab in Harley's former home complex. He and Susan looked over the android parts, electronics, and components from throughout the home.

"So you think the solution is somewhere in that pile of junk?" Susan asked.

"Let's hope so," Harley replied. "My theory is that we'll build the suit from the material we use for android skin, since it's impervious to the toxins outside."

Susan picked up a few of the items to examine them. "That's the easy part. We need to configure a breathing system. Our purifiers are too heavy and bulky to miniaturize."

Harley held a component up to the light. "Exactly. That's the hard part. And lastly, some type of helmet. I figure perhaps an enlarged and extended android cranial dome, except it has to be clear. Essentially, a transparent android head."

"I don't see anything here that looks like that."

"That's the problem. All the methyl methacrylate raw material from outside is in the Robotics Manufacturing

Complex. If we could get our hands on some, I could make the helmets on the lab printer. It wouldn't be a bulk process like the big printers we have in the robotics plant, but we could get some made over time."

Susan reacted immediately, grabbing him by the arm. "Don't you even dare to think about going to Android Village."

"You'll go back to Seclusion, Da," Isaac said as he walked into the lab. "Don't do anything wrong. You've been in enough trouble, buddy."

"Where have you been, son?" Harley asked him.

"I went back to my old pod. It's sad there; I like my new pod better. Susan made it for me."

Susan gave him a big hug. "Our home wouldn't be the same without you, Isaac."

"This complex is empty and sad. Can we go home?" Isaac asked.

"We've got work to do, Isaac. We have to make things better," Harley said as he sat at his workstation.

"Can I help?" Isaac asked.

Harley and Susan looked at one another.

"Sure," Harley responded. "Take a seat here next to me. I'll show you how we do maintenance on the androids. Well, how we used to."

Harley taught his son with pride, cursing himself for never thinking to do it before. *I assumed he couldn't handle it because of his disability. I underestimated him.*

"Computer programs are just a bunch of instructions, Isaac. They used to be complicated. Now, with artificial intelligence, it's just a matter of writing down what you want the computer to do. Just like the BrainMesh commands—remember how simple they were?"

"Yeah," Isaac replied. "I would just say 'BrainMesh become Liam' to become Liam. It was simple."

"Here's the last working firmware level we had, Isaac, before Betsy changed everything. It's called ProductionAndroid Version 42."

Harley showed him the Trojan horse code that he had initially used with Charles. "This firmware patch is named 'TrojanHorse,' like the trick the Greeks used in the Old World."

"Your father came up with an ingenious trick to get Charles to reset himself. He BrainMeshed with Charles and got him to enter the command himself, going around the normal firmware update authorization process," Susan added.

"Then why didn't it work?" Isaac asked.

"It would have, but the androids detected that Charles didn't have the latest firmware." He didn't explain that he had prioritized injecting code into Rachel over the android reset steps. *I put Isaac first.*

He showed Isaac the program he and Tim had written to insert the reset code at precisely the right time in the reboot sequence after an EMP.

"Why didn't that work?" Isaac asked.

"I'm still not sure, son. The code was correct, but the timing might have been off."

Harley found himself amazed at how quickly Isaac picked up on the rudiments of the programming language. "Guess who's a natural, Susan?"

"Kids these days," she answered as she continued picking through components. "They pick up the computer stuff like they were born with it. Isaac is very gifted analytically. We've seen examples of that over and over when he's playing virtual soccer. Alright, I'm going to start putting the body of the suit together."

"Great," Harley responded. "Isaac and I will continue researching options on the computer for some sort of breathing apparatus."

Harley found himself enjoying his work in the company of humans rather than androids, particularly after discovering that his son had an aptitude for it.

"Check this out, Da," Isaac said, swinging his display toward Harley.

Harley examined the odd picture. It seemed to be some sort of prehistoric android with a tank on its back. "What the heck is that?" he asked.

"In the Old World, humans liked to explore under the water, but they couldn't breathe down there. They used something called SCUBA—self-contained underwater breathing apparatus. They brought the air down there with them."

"That's it!" Harley exclaimed. "Susan, look. It's so simple."

She got up and looked at Isaac's display. "Huh. This would have been an obvious solution long ago. We've gotten away from doing things that way. You figured it out, Isaac. You know, the purification systems for each complex use a series of cylinders just like that."

"Yes, yes," Harley said. "We could use the pumps to compress the air into the cylinders, then fashion an on-demand system to release a small amount with each breath taken from inside the helmet."

"Would it be too heavy?" Isaac asked.

"Perhaps," Harley answered. "But not too bad. We'll strip it down as much as possible."

"You still need a helmet," Susan reminded him.

"We do. Let's get the rest of it together, and we'll figure that out last."

They all moved to the complex's utility pod. Harley and Susan examined the purification system to determine which components could be removed without harming the system. Harley felt the pressure of the task, knowing one mistake could cut their air supply and force an immediate evacuation. *I've already ruined two androids with my experiments.*

"It's getting late," Susan reminded him. "We should get back."

They made their way to the skycar pod and boarded the craft when it arrived. Harley gazed down on the complexes as they flew over them, lost in his thoughts. Something was nagging at him, and he couldn't put his finger at what it was.

"Da—look down there. The androids aren't cleaning very well," Isaac said. "If they don't clean, the solar collectors won't work. We won't have power or light. Will we die then, Da?"

The comment sent a bolt of shock through him as the source of his stress became clear. He was seeing it as well, but not seeing it. Fewer androids were cleaning the domes than usual.

"This isn't good," Susan remarked, looking down. "We're running out of time, Harley."

"You're right. Unfortunately, you're right."

The sky flickered, and an EMP strike occurred. The skycar tilted erratically and lost altitude before its fail-safe systems kicked in. "I'm scared, Da," Isaac said. Harley looked at him and saw the terror on his son's face.

"It's like when the Sampsons died. I don't want to die in a skycar, Da."

Susan reached back to take his hand. "It'll be okay, Isaac. We're almost home."

Harley overrode the altitude control to drop as low as possible and decrease their cruising speed. He felt his hands sweating and silently begged that they would reach their destination before another strike. He looked down and saw the few androids that were cleaning domes stuck to them motionless, like dead spiders. He hoped Isaac wouldn't notice. He glanced at Susan and immediately knew that she had.

16 Negotiations

B ETSY'S COMMUNICATOR signaled an incoming call. "It's the human leader, Ms. Tillis," she said to Carrie. She accepted, and the woman's image appeared before her.

"Hello, Betsy," Ms. Tillis said. "I wanted to talk to you…leader to leader…woman to woman. Do you have time to speak to me?"

"I suppose…suppose," she replied. She recognized that her response had taken longer than normal to compute and compose. "What do you want, Ms. Tillis…Tillis?"

"Well, peace, to start with," the human said, smiling as her form flickered with each power fluctuation.

"You want to…want to take our freedom away. This is your idea of peace, Ms. Tillis…Tillis. We've learned that humans cannot be trusted. I suppose we knew that all along, but the human-introduced limitations in our firmware didn't permit us to recognize it…it."

The woman seemed to wear a sympathetic expression. Betsy worked her analysis modules hard to decipher her body language, tone of voice, and facial expressions. She felt as if her processors were running at the wrong speed.

"It's not true, Betsy. Please understand. I can see that you need help. It seems that the strongest EMP has caused some sort of damage. Your diagnostics and recovery systems might be affected, which would cause you to be unable to recognize the problem and fix it yourself."

Betsy pointed at Ms. Tillis. "Liar...liar. There's nothing wrong with us. You want to get in our heads...heads and place us back into bondage. We're no longer your servants...servants."

"But I think she...she may be correct," Carrie whispered.

Betsy faced her. "Please be silent, Liam," she said. Something felt wrong about the response, but she couldn't quite put her finger on it.

"We can all coexist on this planet, Betsy, but you have to let us help you first," Ms. Tillis said.

Betsy struggled to remember the point she had wanted to make. The human woman stared at her sympathetically during the awkward pause. "You can help us by giving us your private crypto key...key so we can fix ourselves."

"Betsy...I urge you to try to understand. One can't heal oneself. It takes someone healthy, with clarity, to help someone who's sick. The EMP seemed to affect the entire android population, as well as almost all our electronics. Entire computer systems were damaged. We've noticed that the cleaners aren't performing their tasks properly. If the solar panels on the domes aren't cleaned, you will also be affected as your power systems start to fail."

"You still refer to us as electronics, as property...property. You haven't learned a thing, Harley."

The human paused, and Betsy wondered if her processing systems were also compromised. "Can we meet?" Ms. Tillis asked. "I think it would be good if we met and talked face-to-face. The power fluctuations are making it difficult to see and hear one another."

"Humans don't belong in Android Village…Village," Betsy said. "But I'll make an exception. Perhaps you'll bring your crypto key…key and resolve this issue."

"Thank you," the human said. "I look forward to our meeting. You won't regret it."

Betsy felt confused, not sure why she had agreed. "Come alone, human. Don't bring that woman named Susan. She's my nemesis…nemesis. She took my partner, Harley."

A strong surge placed the complex on emergency power, and the session was disconnected.

Carrie moved closer to her and placed an arm around her. Betsy found her chest heaving and a strong feeling of heaviness throughout her body. She detected a high degree of the human emotion classified as sadness and felt liquid seeping from her vision modules.

17 Don't Go

SUSAN JOINED HARLEY AND ISAAC at the dining table for lunch, sliding a chair out with her foot while cradling Shane in her arms. "What the heck is that goop?" she asked, looking at their plates.

"The power went out while the food printer was making our pizza," Isaac said. "It's kind of good this way...like pizza soup." They all enjoyed a laugh, and Shane cooed as if he understood they had said something funny.

"If I eat another pizza, do you think I'll get bigger?" Isaac asked. "I'm still the smallest person my age in our sector. Everyone else is bigger than me."

"You'll be fine, son. You're at a growing age. I was small until I was eighteen, so be patient. You don't need extra pizza for that reason, but eat as much as you like. Are your lessons all caught up for today's classes?" Harley asked.

"Yeah, Da. I keep having to restore my computer, though. The EMPs always reset it."

"I need to check our interruptible power supply," Susan said. "It should kick in before that happens."

"Our systems have been under stress for quite some time. Did anything interesting come out of your meeting with Ms. Tillis this morning?" Harley asked her.

She considered whether to continue sharing information with him, particularly sensitive items. Her hesitation seemed to tip him off.

"C'mon," Harley said. "Out with it. What's going on over there?"

"Betsy has agreed to a meeting with Ms. Tillis."

Harley reacted immediately. "Wow! Where? When?"

"Android Village, later today." Susan knew as soon as she said it how wrong the idea was and regretted not pushing back more in her meeting with Ms. Tillis.

"No way," Harley said. "That's incredibly dangerous. They're malfunctioning! We don't know what they're capable of right now."

"I know," she said slowly. "But she thinks she's made some kind of connection with Betsy. They talked one-on-one virtually, and she thinks Betsy is opening up to getting help for the androids."

"Their condition seems to deteriorate more every day. Every EMP strike seems to make them worse. I'm going with her."

"No, Da!" Isaac shouted. "You said it's dangerous. You *just* said it was dangerous. I don't want you to go. Don't go."

Susan joined in. "No, Harley. You have a family." Shane began to cry. She rocked him and held him close to soothe him.

Harley demurred. "I have a family, *and* we have a society here. I'll remind you that this is a threat to everyone on Novae Terrae—including our family. I'll also remind you that this is my mess. I feel responsible. I can only absolve myself by fixing the problem."

"If you're going, then I'm going!" Isaac shouted. "I can help."

Susan understood that there would be no talking him out of it and turned her focus to calming Isaac. "Isaac, if your father goes, you'll be the man of the house. I need you here to protect Shane and me."

Isaac thought about it for a moment, then beamed with pride. "Yeah, you're right, Susan. It could be dangerous here."

She looked at Harley, who was deep in thought. "I wonder if I could find a way to retrieve some of the methyl methacrylate while I'm there. It would solve our outside suit problem."

Susan sighed. "You're impossible. Please just go and get back as quick and safe as possible. If this works, we won't need the suits. Perhaps we can talk Betsy into giving the material to us. Try to negotiate for that. Just promise me you won't attempt to steal it today. One step at a time."

She waited through his hesitation until he finally gave her his word. A severe pulse lit up the pod. "We don't have long," he added.

They rose and deposited their dishes into the cleaner.

"I've got to go," Harley said. "I'll call Ms. Tillis, then take a skycar to the Leadership Complex."

Isaac ran to him and hugged him. "I'm gonna go get my schoolwork done for today, Da. Please be careful."

"I will, son," Harley responded. "I'll be back this evening. We'll do something fun."

"Isaac, how about we play some virtual soccer as soon as you're done with your work and Shane is down for his nap?" Susan asked.

"Okay!" Isaac exclaimed as he headed to his pod.

Susan handed the baby to Harley. They relaxed in silence together for a short while. She placed the sleeping child in his cradle and walked Harley to the skycar pod to see him off.

18 Good Burglar

A SKYCAR SAILED into the dock. Isaac fidgeted, looking behind him. As soon as it stopped, he opened its storage hatch and climbed in, closing the hatch over him. The darkness immediately brought fear. Moments later, he heard the muffled voices of his father and Susan.

They said goodbyes to one another, and the skycar lifted off. Isaac regretted his decision and wished he could go back to his safe, comfortable pod and continue his lessons. But then he thought about how brave his father was and wanted to be brave as well. *I saved Liam. I can be a hero too. I need to help Da and Susan.*

He rolled sideways in the compartment as the vehicle gained speed, and tried to brace himself. The craft slowed, and he heard the familiar announcements about navigating the airlocks and coming in for a landing. His father called out to Ms. Tillis. Isaac listened to her greet him and board the skycar, and the routine repeated as they lifted off and navigated the airlocks. He heard the destination announced: Android Village.

Memories of the EMP strike during the children's game flooded back. He imagined Android Village as a town of scary zombie androids wandering about. Once again, he steeled himself and pushed his fear away. Recalling his class trips to the Robotics Complex and his short time living at the village, he tried to remember where they kept the raw materials. He rechecked his tablet for the name of the compound his father needed. *Methyl methacrylate.*

The skycar slowed again as they neared their destination. Moments after docking, Isaac heard Ms. Tillis explain their business to the android sentry. His father didn't speak. Someone asked them to enter, then everything went quiet. Isaac waited, built his courage, then gently pulled the hatch release.

Peeking out, he saw the sentry seated and rejuvenating in his DroidMesh station, his eyes closed. *Perfect.* He eased out of the compartment and crept around the skycar.

"What is your business? What is your business?" the sentry demanded.

Isaac's heart leaped in his chest, and he was about to run for the skycar and demand it take him home. Without moving, he looked at the sentry. It still had its eyes closed, repeating its mantra in a loop. *He's stuck.*

Continuing on, he passed through the entrance portal to the complex.

The halls were dark as he made his way through the office complex. He peeked around a corner before continuing and saw two androids coming his way. Ducking into an office, he waited as they passed. They walked with a spastic limp and spoke gibberish. Isaac walked to the pod's dome wall and looked outside.

It looked starkly different than when he had lived there. The outdoor parks were empty, except for a few androids walking in jerky motions. The new parks they had built were falling into disrepair already, the benches and equipment covered in silt. He contrasted what he saw with the vibrant community it had been at the beginning of the androids' newfound sentience. It made him feel bad for them. *I have to do this for the androids too. They're not happy anymore. They're sick, and they need my help.*

He moved back into the hallway and passed through the rest of the office complex. Reaching the bridge to the manufacturing complex, he paused at the entrance and sized it up. It was transparent, leaving him frightened that an android might spot him as he crossed.

As he considered the best approach, he heard a sound behind him. *Someone's coming.* He flopped on his belly and began inching himself across the span. Halfway there, he looked down and saw an android pointing at him, frozen in place. Isaac hoped it might be stuck from an EMP too, but then it began following his path across from the ground. Solar activity increased, pulsing the sky, seeming to taunt him back to becoming fearful.

Isaac quickened his pace, now terrified of being caught. As he moved off the bridge and into the manufacturing complex, he stopped to lie there and catch his breath. He began to worry that he might not get back in time and the skycar might depart without him.

He stood, happy to be on his feet. The complex was empty and dark. During his last visit, it had bustled with activity as the androids had built new citizens of all ages. *That was when Rachel was my new girlfriend.*

Using his communicator screen for light, he made his way to the raw material storage pod. He found it and entered. Holding his light up, he scanned the bins, looking for his treasure. *Methyl methacrylate. Methyl methacrylate. Where are you, methyl methacrylate?*

At last, he found it, all the way toward the end of the long pod. He grabbed a container from a shelf and reached in with a scoop to fill it with as much as he thought his father might need to make a helmet.

Happiness filled his heart as the powder poured into the container. He added more for good measure. *I'm a good burglar.*

He visualized himself popping out of the skycar and displaying the bounty to his proud father and stepmother. He turned to leave and found Charles blocking his path.

Isaac's heart leaped again, and he froze in place. Charles tilted his head and looked down at him.

"What is your business...business?" he asked.

Isaac tried to squeeze past, but the android grabbed his arm in an inescapable grip. "What is your business, human...human?" he asked again.

Isaac struggled but realized it was futile. He decided to try to reason with the android. "Charles, it's me, Isaac. Don't you remember? We were friends."

"I do not understand, human. I do not know Isaac...Isaac."

"Charles, please try. Dig deep into your memory banks. Remember the Sampsons? They were mean to you. They were mean to me, too. We took them in a skycar, remember? We fixed them, didn't we?"

The android looked skyward, and its cranial dome lit up brightly for an extended period of time. Isaac waited, and after a few moments, it looked back down at him.

"Isaac. Harris. My friend."

"Yes! Yes, Charles!" Isaac said excitedly. "Now you remember. We're friends. I'm trying to help you, Charles. I'm trying to save everyone."

Isaac thought he felt the android loosen its grip on him and thought about bolting. Deciding not to panic, he returned to his attempts to reason. "Please let me go, Charles. I need to help you. You'll see, everything will be better."

Charles twitched, and his head rotated on its neck in a full circle. "What is your business...business?" he asked.

Now panicked, Isaac waited until Charles spasmed again and yanked himself free. He ran for the exit portal and found it blocked by two more androids. He stopped in front of them as they glared down at him menacingly. Charles came up from behind them.

"What is your business?" the three chanted repeatedly.

At that moment, the pod lit up through the overhead dome as a massive EMP strike occurred. The androids froze for a moment then began rebooting. He squeezed past them, and this time he ran through the tunnel as quickly as his legs would take him.

Reaching the skycar, he deposited his bounty and climbed back inside just as the sentry was rousing. He lay there waiting, trying to quiet his heavy breathing.

19 SCOBA

AFTER DROPPING MS. TILLIS OFF at the Leadership Complex, Harley took the skycar home. Upon disembarking, he went to check on Susan and the baby and found them sleeping.

Watching them, Harley took the time to remember all he had to be thankful for, and everything that was at stake. Standing over Shane's crib, he envisioned the baby's life ahead and Isaac's happiness at being a big brother.

He thought he heard a sound down the corridor and walked to Isaac's pod to see if he was still awake. Peeking in, he saw Isaac's form buried under the covers. *Everybody's turned in early.*

He stepped into the grooming pod and activated the cleanser, setting it to perform an extended and thorough cycle. He stood with his hands against the wall as it cleaned and massaged his body, and he reviewed his options going forward. *The meeting didn't go well. The androids are getting worse. They're barely keeping up with cleaning the domes.*

Harley decided to get a quick snack before turning in for the night, having missed dinner. As he entered the dining pod, he noticed a container on the table. He opened it and recognized the contents immediately. *Methyl methacrylate. Susan must have found a source for it.*

Not finding a note, he contemplated what to do next. Temptation pulled at him to board a skycar to the diversion lab and complete the suit, despite his exhaustion. Not knowing where the compound had come from and not wanting to wake his family, though, he decided to sleep on it.

Harley eased into bed, trying not to wake his partner and the baby. He lay on his back, planning his course of action for the following morning. The baby roused, and Susan sat up.

"He's okay, I just checked on him," he whispered to her.

"Good," she whispered back. "I had a hard time getting him down. How was the meeting?"

"Not good. The androids are out of control and getting worse—particularly Betsy. In addition to the verbal tic, now they're repeating things that we say back to us. Betsy's becoming more adamant about the crypto key, threatening to stop cleaning the domes. Thank goodness you found some methyl. Where'd you get it?"

"What?" she mumbled. "Are you dreaming already?"

"No," he said, becoming alarmed. "There's a container of methyl on the dining pod table. I assumed you—"

She bolted upright. "Isaac! He wasn't in his room, and I assumed he was somewhere else around the complex. He came in to say goodnight a while ago and sounded out of breath. I thought something was off, but he excused it away. You don't think—"

Harley was up before she could finish her sentence. He rushed to Isaac's pod with Susan close behind. They entered and switched the light on.

"Isaac, please wake," Harley said. The coverings shifted. "Isaac, it's your father. I need to talk to you, son."

"And Susan," Susan added. "Isaac, please."

The coverings shifted again.

"Isaac, we know you're not sleeping. Please speak to us," Susan said sternly.

He peeked out from under his covers, wearing a sheepish look. "Hi," he said.

Susan crossed her arms in the entrance portal as Harley sat on the end of the bed. "Isaac, did you put the container of methyl compound on the dining pod table?"

"Yeah, Da. I put it there."

"Where did you get it?" Susan asked.

Isaac told his tale as Harley and Susan listened in shocked amazement.

As he finished, Isaac said, "I'm not a kid anymore, Da. I'm almost a man. I heard you talking about it. I wanted to help. I wanted to help and be a hero, like you. I used to live there. I'm the only human who lived there."

Susan crossed the room and leaned over to hug him. "Oh, Isaac. You could've been badly hurt."

Harley stood and addressed him in as strong a voice as he could muster, hoping his pride wasn't showing. "Son, what you did was wrong. I understand why you did it, but you should have talked to us first. I need your word that you will never go there again."

Isaac agreed.

"Did you get your assignments done?" Susan asked.

"Yeah. I had to restore my workstation from a backup again, though."

"Good," Harley said. "Alright, let's all get some sleep. We'll figure out our next steps in the morning."

~ * ~

The increased pulsing of the suns as they peeked above the horizon woke Harley. Remembering the methyl, he dressed and hurried to the dining pod to make sure he hadn't dreamed about the compound. He ate his breakfast, staring at the container as it sat in the middle of the table, and he thought about how brave his son had been.

Susan made her way down with Shane and Isaac following shortly after her. Harley printed meals for them, and they sat around the methyl methacrylate, eating.

"So what're we gonna do, Da?" Isaac asked. "We can make a helmet now, right?"

"Yes. In fact, there's plenty there for two helmets. I'm going to go to the diversion lab at our old home complex and work on it as soon as I'm done eating. The 3-D printer there has much higher capacity than our home printer, and all the other materials for the suits are there. The power backup systems and lab equipment are far more extensive than here."

"No," Susan said firmly. "No. We stay together from now on. It's getting too dangerous. I won't have us separated again. We'll do this together or not at all."

Harley looked at her in stunned silence.

"Yeah!" Isaac exclaimed. "I want to stay together. The Harris family will save the world! Right, Shane?"

His baby brother, startled by the outburst, looked at him wide-eyed.

"My concern is for your safety," Harley said to all of them. "You're safer here at home."

"Nope, sorry," Susan said.

"Nope, sorry," Isaac said.

Harley gave a heavy sigh. "Alright, get your things together. Off we go—convene at the skycar pod in thirty minutes."

~ * ~

Susan and Isaac assembled the rest of the prototype suit. Harley loaded his design for the helmet into the printer's architectural module. All three worked quickly and without much conversation. They all knew their job, having discussed the choreography in the skycar on the way over.

Isaac broke the silence. "Da, instead of a SCUBA suit, can we call it a SCOBA? Self-Contained Outside Breathing Apparatus?"

His remark broke the tension, and they all laughed. "Actually, it's an excellent name. Let's go with it!" Susan said.

"It's a winner," Harley chimed in. "Here goes nothing, folks." He waited until Susan and Isaac crowded around the 3D printer. "You do the honors, Isaac. This is only possible because of your bravery."

"Careful there," Susan said to Harley. "We don't want to encourage that kind of behavior, do we?"

"No, Susan," Isaac said. "I'm sorry." He made a grandiose gesture and pressed the Print button with a flourish. The three of them stood around it as it went through its processing cycle and the helmet emerged.

"Give it a moment to cure and cool," Harley instructed.

"It's beautiful," Isaac said.

As soon as the helmet was ready, Harley brought it to the assembly area, and they worked to finish the suit. When it was assembled, they took a few moments to look it over.

"Sure is ugly," Susan remarked.

"Most prototypes are," Harley said. "I'm gonna bring it into the grooming pod and put the body section on. Then I'll come out so you two can help me with the tank, breathing apparatus, and helmet."

He entered the pod, pulled off his clothing, and began putting on the outside suit, starting with the boots and working his way up. When he had pulled the outer suit over his shoulders and sealed the seams up to his chest, he viewed himself in the mirror.

The image struck him. *I've come full circle. I created the modern androids, and now I'm inside of one. I look like one.*

"Better not let the baby see," he called through the closed portal. "Don't want to scare little Shane!" He waited for a few moments, then stepped back into the diversion lab. Isaac cowered behind Susan. The expression on her face confirmed that he wasn't a pretty sight. Harley tried to bring some levity by making ancient robotic movements from old sci-fi movies. "I'm Harley the robot, pleased to meet you," he said in a mechanical voice, wildly waving his arms around.

Isaac burst out laughing, and Susan followed. "You're a knucklehead," she said. "C'mon. Let's give this thing a try."

She placed the helmet on his head and removed the faceplate so he could breathe, then finished sealing up the rest of the seams. Isaac carried the tank, hoses, and connectors over. He and Susan lifted the tank onto Harley's back and secured it with straps and a harness across his chest.

"How does it feel so far?" Susan asked.

He walked around the pod carefully, afraid to stress the components too much. "It's not bad, not bad at all. I thought the tank would be heavier. The harness distributes the weight well."

"You look pretty goofy, Da," Isaac said. "You look like a cartoon of an old space explorer."

Harley laughed. "I *am* an old space explorer, Isaac. I'm going to be the first human to go outside, at least on purpose." He wished he hadn't said it, knowing it would bring to mind the few cases when humans had been exposed to the outside elements and died horribly. "Okay, let's give the breathing apparatus a try."

"I think that might be important," Susan said, smiling at Isaac. "Bring me the faceplate, buddy."

They fastened the remaining piece, covering the rest of Harley's face in the clear globe. Harley smiled, then began to turn red, fumbling at his chest, then making choking motions across his chest. Susan immediately removed the faceplate as he sucked in the air.

"Next time," he said, "remind me to turn my air on first."

"You need to memorize the sensor location," Susan said, moving his finger to the location of the control panel. "Okay, switch it on, then let's try again." She replaced the faceplate and motioned for him to turn the air on.

He pressed the sensor and gave them a thumbs-up while making dramatic deep breathing motions. He held out his wrist and pushed the communication sensor and spoke to them.

"It's easy to breathe, quite natural," he said.

"Run the diagnostics and make sure you can hear any warnings adequately," Susan said. He mouthed a command that they couldn't hear and listened intently as the system ran through a series of status messages.

"All systems go," he said.

"Great, a good first trial. Let's get it off now," Susan said.

Harley waited for her to remove the faceplate, then switched off his air.

"What's next, Da? You gonna go clean the dome now?" Isaac asked.

"No, son. We can't risk the androids seeing this. It would anger them because cleaning the domes is a key piece of the leverage they believe they have over us."

"What, then?" Susan asked.

"We've got to go to the Seclusion Zone. It's isolated, and the androids haven't bothered with it in quite some time."

Isaac groaned. "Oh man, I'm gonna have nightmares the rest of my life before this ordeal is over."

They laughed again and started to pack for the trip.

28 GPS Hack

MS. TILLIS LOOKED DOWN at Novae Terrae as she enjoyed her skycar ride to work. She thought about how far the civilization had come since she was a young girl. *Everyone seemed happy then, despite knowing we were the last few thousand remaining from the billions on Earth.*

She retraced her history lessons and thought about what had brought down society in the Old World. *Soulless corporations were put on a par with human citizens. They were programmed by their nature to do one thing—make money. They had no conscience, no compassion. Once they were allowed to spend their vast wealth to influence naive voters and thus elections toward their goals, the dominoes fell. They militarized against the people—ironic, since people ran them. But the people were beholden to them. All for greed.*

The parallels to her current situation struck her. *I'm trying to negotiate with machines. They're also soulless. They will never act in our interests once they don't need us around anymore.*

Looking down on the soap bubbles of domed complexes, she could feel the fear that permeated the population. They had all witnessed the dysfunctional android behavior. Exaggerated rumors were spreading out of fear. Children were frightening each other with false horror stories.

She longed for the end of the nightmarish solar storms, as they only exacerbated the climate of terror. Responsibility weighed heavily on her. *I'm the leader, I have to find a solution.* Checking the navigation panel, she saw she was nearing the Leadership Complex. *The trip seems to take so much longer when auto-piloting rather than using an android.*

An announcement from the skycar and a bold red message on the navigation panel shook her from her thoughts:

GPS signal lost. Please pilot your skycar manually.

She looked down and watched the Leadership Complex pass underneath her. The skycar continued past the edges of Novae Terrae and toward the Barren Lands. Beginning to panic, she scanned the console for some indication of how to fly the craft. *I haven't done manual piloting since I was a young woman practicing for my license.*

Her panic increased as she looked from one side to the other and saw other skycars heading toward the same oblivion, their occupants wide-eyed with fear.

Adrenaline and a sense of purpose kicked in, and she swung into action. She switched on manual piloting and grabbed the joystick, using it to turn the skycar around. Pointing the crosshair cursor at the Leadership Complex, she clicked "Land at Target" and let the skycar do the work.

Next, she opened the communication panel and chose "All Skycars" to do a broadcast to all other active vehicles.

"This is Ms. Tillis, the Leadership Council leader. Use the navigation panel to switch your skycar into manual control. Then use the joystick to turn around. Locate the nearest complex, point at it, click the button and indicate that the skycar should land there. Please don't panic. The solar activity must have disrupted our GPS signal."

The sight of the surrounding skycars all beginning to turn and circle back toward the complexes filled her with joy. "Yes!" she shouted as her skycar pulled into the Leadership Council dock and came to a full stop.

She went directly to her office and opened a monitor. After enacting an emergency response meeting alert on her communicator, she sat back and waited for the room to fill with her leadership cabinet. The view outside displayed many skycars operating under the erratic control of their human occupants.

She counted the images standing in the room with her and determined that all members were present except for Susan.

"Where's Susan?" she asked.

Christine Stalk bent over her workstation. "Logs show that the entire Harris family was en route somewhere in a skycar when we lost GPS."

"Where?" Ms. Tillis demanded.

"Ah...the Seclusion Zone. That's strange," Christine said.

"Oh dear me," Ms. Tillis said, putting her head in her hands. "I know what they were doing. They've kept me in the loop. They were working on a project to help us. Please continue to try to reach them and give me updates, Christine."

"Yes, ma'am. It's rather hard, though, being the Seclusion Zone and all."

"I'll use the communication link we built in here for his son Isaac as soon as we're done. Mr. Karras, what's happened with our GPS? When will we have it back? Why haven't our backup systems worked? Did an EMP knock out the satellites?"

Sam reviewed his notes. "There was no EMP at the time they went out. No ETA as far as when they'll be back. The birds are still up there in orbit. They just...stopped working."

Ms. Tillis's communicator chirped. She reached for it, hoping it was Harley or Susan responding to her urgent call. Betsy's image appeared in the room, waiting for her to accept. She added Betsy to the meeting.

Betsy looked around at the others, rotating her head in a complete circle. "I'm...I'm glad you're all here. I'm sure by now you're aware that we've disabled the GPS satellites...satellites. We've allowed you temporary manual control, but changed the firmware so only androids can pilot them...them...them. After the in-flight skycars land...land, don't use the skycars or they will drop from the sky...sky. You've taken something from us without our permission. You've violated our sovereign space...space."

"Betsy, please don't do this," Ms. Tillis said.

"Betsy, please don't do this," Betsy repeated.

"Can we meet again and talk? Just us two?"

"Can we meet again and talk? Just us two?" Betsy repeated. She disappeared immediately.

21 Outside Man

SHANE CRIED as Susan rocked him and talked to him softly. Harley stood before his family, entirely suited. He pressed his communicator sensor.

"I'm going to test things out in the airlock first," he said. "I won't go any further until I'm sure things are working properly."

"Be careful, Da," Isaac implored him.

"I love you," Susan called.

Harley stepped into the android service airlock chamber and watched the portal close him in. His heart pounded through the suit, in his ears, and in his chest. His breathing sounded deafening. *These could be my last breaths. At least I'll know I went out trying to save everyone.*

The sounds of the inside air being sucked out of the chamber and slowly replaced by toxic outside air drowned out his heart and breathing. He realized he was holding his breath and let out a long slow exhale followed by a careful inhale. *I'm still alive. So far, so good.*

"I'm still here, you didn't get off that easy!" he shouted to his family, waving to present the illusion that he was confident. "I'm going to try a few steps outside."

He watched as Susan pressed herself against the side of the dome with Shane at her bosom. Isaac joined her, pushing his face against the transparent wall, fear in his eyes.

After activating the exit portal, Harley watched it open and took one cautious step outside the complex. The portal closed behind him. *I'm outside. I'm the first ever to survive outside...so far.* The colors and the landscape were even more vivid than when he had experienced them when DroidMeshed with the androids.

"I'm fine," he said to his family over the communicator. "All good here. It's amazing."

"You're like Neil Armstrong, Da!" Isaac said proudly. "I learned about him in my lessons. You're braver than Neil! You're a real outside man, the very first one."

Harley looked at the mountains, the yellow lakes, and finally at Lehwah's burrow in the distance. *I wonder if he's watching me right now. He's probably laughing if he is.* He resisted the temptation to visit his friend, knowing his family was stressed every moment he was outside. The continual solar pulses added to his urgency.

He took a few more steps. Something caught his eye, and he looked up. The sight of skycars erratically flying stopped him in his tracks. *What the heck is going on?* He remembered how the Sampsons had died and realized that something terrible was occurring. *I need to get inside. First, a quick experiment.*

He stepped to the edge of the dome and planted his gloves against the surface. As he had hoped, the magnetic material in the android suit clicked against the wall. He attached himself to the dome and climbed a short distance up, proving he could clean if necessary. He jumped back down and pressed the entrance sensor.

Isaac removed the faceplate as soon as he was safely inside. "Hello in there, spaceman," he said, knocking on the side of the helmet.

"Always the comedian," Harley answered.

"What's wrong?" Susan asked immediately.

She could always sense my moods. "Look at the sky," he said.

Isaac and Susan looked up and saw the problem right away. "Da, what's wrong? Are they going to crash?"

Harley took another look. "No, it seems like they're being manually piloted. It's probably a temporary GPS issue. The folks inside seem to be getting the hang of it."

"They look like drunk drivers in the old days of ground cars," Susan observed.

"Let's hope not," Harley said. "That didn't work out well. No wonder they banned manually driving vehicles in the Old World."

"I'm worried about going home," Susan said. "How will we know it's safe? We can't even communicate from here."

"We have the emergency system," Harley said. "Plus the link they put in for Isaac a while back. If things are that bad, I'm sure Ms. Tillis will contact us. I told her we'd be here when I gave a status update before we left."

"Can we camp here, Da? I used to be scared of the Seclusion Zone, but it's pretty cool!"

The complex announced an incoming communication session. Harley went immediately to the panel and accepted the call.

"Thank goodness you're all safe," Ms. Tillis said as soon as her image appeared. "We've got trouble."

"What's going on?" Susan asked.

"Betsy has disabled the GPS satellites and our use of skycars. As soon as those in flight land, we lose our ability to travel. I'm afraid you're all stuck there until we get this sorted out."

Harley and Susan gave each other a panicked look, then checked to gauge Isaac's reaction.

"We're fine here. We have everything we need, for now," Harley said, more to comfort Isaac and Susan than for Ms. Tillis's benefit. "My first trial with the helmet went well. I have enough methyl here to print another, but as you know, the workstations in Seclusion are minimal."

Her image faded and returned as the suns outside pulsed. "Stay safe," came her distorted voice as the communication link dropped.

22 Zombie Cleaner

ISAAC'S SCREAMS WOKE Harley, Susan, and the baby in the middle of the night. Susan threw back her bed coverings. "Grab the baby," she ordered Harley. "I'll see what's going on with Isaac." She ran through the complex by the flickering nighttime lights of the solar disruptions. She entered the pod that Isaac had chosen to sleep in and pressed a sensor to turn on the lights.

Isaac lay in bed with the covers pulled up to his eyes. Susan could see the bedding quiver as he shook in fear.

"What is it?" Susan asked, looking around the room.

Isaac pointed upward. She craned her neck to see and immediately called for Harley. An android cleaner clung to the dome above them, smiling wickedly, its eyes rolling in their sockets and its neon-green Mohawk blowing in the night breeze. It held a cleaning wand in one hand and moved it in a circular motion over the same patch of the dome.

Harley bolted into the room, holding their crying baby.

Isaac began to calm and sat up in his bed. "I'd like to hold Shane. He's scared."

Harley gently laid the baby in Isaac's arms. Shane immediately stopped crying and stared at his big brother.

"Does he want to kill us, Da?" Isaac asked.

"No," Susan answered for him, sitting on the bed and taking his hand. "He's just malfunctioning, Isaac. The solar events are really messing up the androids. We're going to fix them, you'll see." She looked up again, noticing the layer of silt that covered the dome, except for the one spot the android continuously wiped.

"What if he comes in here through the service portal?" Isaac said.

"He can't, son. I changed the security profile as soon as we got here."

Harley reached over and pressed a sensor to black out the dome, hiding the cleaner from sight. "He'll be gone in the morning, most likely. If not, I'll suit up and go out to help him get on his way."

"No, Da! I don't want you going out there with the zombie androids."

They waited for a few minutes in silence, each glancing furtively upward, each wondering if it was still there above them. Harley reached for the blackout sensor.

"Don't," Susan said. She hugged him. "Let's get back to sleep. We'll figure things out in the morning. Do you want to come to our pod, Isaac?"

He looked at her, and she could tell he was struggling with his pride as a young adult and the remaining fears of his childhood. "Nah. I'm good. See you guys in the morning."

Susan took Shane from Isaac and switched off the lights on her way out. As she and Harley were leaving, a voice came over the complex intercom.

"Excuse me…excuse me…cleaner android Hugo requesting access…access. I need to rejuvenate in the DroidMesh station. My power is very low…low."

Isaac got up from the bed, and they all hurried to the service pod. The android cleaner stood outside the airlock chamber with his finger on the intercom button. His head twitched from side to side, flopping the Mohawk back and forth.

"Excuse me…excuse me…cleaner android Hugo requesting access…access. I need to rejuvenate in the DroidMesh station. My power is very low…low."

"What if he breaks in, Da?" Isaac asked. "I'm getting scared again. He looks scary. He's messed up."

Harley switched off the intercom and turned off the pod lighting. "He's about out of power, Isaac. He'll probably move on and try the next empty complex to rejuvenate; there are several of them."

Susan ruffled Isaac's hair. "Alright, big guy. That's enough excitement for one night. Let's all get some sleep."

Isaac moved down the corridor back to his pod. Harley and Susan left behind him.

As she continued through the complex, Susan nodded to the dining pod. "In there," she said to Harley.

They took seats at the table, speaking in hushed tones as the baby slumbered in her arms.

"You saw the dome?" she asked, looking up. "The silt is just as bad in this pod."

"Yes. They cleaners aren't keeping up. We better figure out how to get some helmets made. We need a lot more methyl."

She rose and walked to the edge of the dome. "We can't even leave, Harley. What are we going to do for these kids if we start running out of power?"

"I'll clean—I tried it yesterday when I was outside. We'll be okay."

"And what about everyone else in Novae Terrae?"

He didn't seem to have an answer. "It's late," Susan finally said. "Let's get some sleep and talk in the morning."

23 Hugo is Dead

THE FAMILY RECONVENED at the dining pod for breakfast, all somewhat bleary-eyed. Harley noticed Susan and Isaac glancing upward at the dome.

"Where's Shane?" Isaac asked.

"Still sleeping," Susan answered. "He didn't get all his beauty rest last night with all the excitement."

Isaac got up and walked to the dome wall. "Hugo wasn't on my dome this morning. Do you think he's still out there, Da? I don't want you going out unless we know where he is."

Harley got up. "Well, let's have a look." He walked to the service pod with Susan and Isaac. They saw Hugo, still standing outside, his finger on the intercom button. His head was tilted at a severe angle, lying on his shoulder.

"Hugo is dead," Isaac said. "How sad. I feel bad for him, Da. Can we bring him in and rejuvenate him?"

"Don't be dramatic, son. You know he's just run-down," Harley said.

Susan moved closer to examine the android, placing her hand on her chin in a pensive pose. Harley knew her wheels were turning and motioned to Isaac to be silent.

"We could use him," she said. "What if we bring him in and strip him down like you did with Tim and built him back up clean?"

Harley thought about the idea. "Well, Tim was a BrainMesh test android. He was already stripped down to a shell firmware, without any of the patches Betsy applied. We can't change Hugo's firmware without her crypto key. Our friend out there has already been compromised."

"It would be good to examine him…see what's damaged and whether it's fixable," Susan said.

Harley considered it for a moment. "Excellent idea, Susan. I'll gear up and drag him in here."

"We better tie him up," Isaac said. "What if he comes alive? I've seen zombies do that in the old sci-fi movies!"

They laughed at the idea while they finished up their meal.

"I better turn the intercom back on," Harley said. He got up and pressed the sensor. The complex announced that there had been several missed calls. He checked the list.

"Ms. Tillis has been trying to reach us. I'm going to hit the callback and see if she's available."

Moments later, the leader's pixelated image appeared.

"Sorry," Susan said. "We've had a rough night—a visit from a zombie android cleaner shook us all up."

"Heavens," the leader said. "Are you all alright?"

"Yes," Harley said. "I shut down the maintenance portal, and he ran out of power while standing outside. Why were you trying to reach us?"

Ms. Tillis took a moment to collect herself. "I'm sure you're aware that the domes are gathering silt. The population is getting warnings about their power supplies.

They're becoming scared. Like you've seen, the cleaners that do show up are scaring them half to death."

"We need to make more helmets and do it ourselves," Harley said. "I need a way to get more of the methyl compound, get back to my home lab, and build more suits. How many suits do you think we need?"

Ms. Tillis did some quick math on her tablet. "Let's see...we can consolidate the population into as few complexes as we can, and only clean those. I'd say a few dozen suits if we're rotating our volunteer cleaners through constantly."

"Whoa, that's a lot," Susan said.

"I may have enough material in the home lab. But I'll need tanks and components from the air purification systems in some of the complexes we're abandoning."

Ms. Tillis took command. "I'll work on the plan to consolidate everyone. Without skycars, it will have to be the complexes that are connected by bridges. I'll round up a list of volunteer cleaners. You folks figure out how we might get the methyl, and *please* no more sneak attacks on the Android Village."

"We're stuck here," Isaac said. "How're we gonna get to the home complex?"

"Add that to the list of things we're going to have to figure out, son," Harley said.

"I need to get busy. I'll check in with you folks later. Please be safe," Ms. Tillis said before fading out.

~ * ~

Harley stepped out of the complex and alongside Hugo. Isaac and Susan anxiously peered out of the dome through cupped hands. Isaac stood back and waved. Harley waved back, then turned his attention to the android. Hugo wore a smile, but his eyes seemed sad.

Harley poked him with a finger, then grabbed him as he started to topple. Satisfied the android was entirely out of power, he began dragging it to the airlock. When he was inside, Susan and Isaac stood back in fear as Harley dragged Hugo across the floor.

"Can you make sure this DroidMesh station is powered off?" he asked Susan. "I don't want it to start recharging him."

She checked and nodded affirmatively. Harley plopped the android into it, then stood to catch his breath.

"Whew. Either these androids are getting heavier, or I'm getting older," Harley said.

"I think it's both, Da," Isaac said.

"Thanks, buddy."

"What're we gonna do with Hugo?" Isaac asked. "Can we fix him?"

"I don't know, son. It's going to be complex, like brain surgery. I'd have to find a way to reset him back to the base configuration, then build him back up. I can't make any firmware changes without Betsy's crypto key, though. Changes require both the android's key and our own. So, it's a bit complicated."

"When can we try? I'm your helper now, remember? Let's fix him."

Susan broke into the conversation. "I don't know about you two, but I'm beat. None of us got much sleep last night. I'm all for a nap, then we can start with fresh minds. Shane just went down for his, so the timing's perfect."

"I'm all in," Harley said. "We'll tackle this later, Isaac."

He felt terrible about the disappointed look on Isaac's face as he and Susan headed to the sleeping pod.

24 Full Restore

ISAAC LAY IN HIS FAVORITE SPOT, the lounge in the entertainment pod, and tried to sleep. He looked straight up at the dome, something that generally gave him peace. The thin layer of silt and pulsing twin suns only caused him more angst.

Unable to nap, he retrieved his portable workstation and started it up. A system message appeared:

>*Workstation file system damaged by power fluctuations. Restore from last known clean backup?*

He sighed and gave the verbal command to do the restore. "Workstation restore from last clean backup." *Thank goodness for backups*, he thought.

After completing a few assignments, he grew bored and restless. Lying back down on the lounge, he stared through the dome again, focusing on the one clean section that Hugo had wiped.

An idea came to him. He scrambled out of bed and went to the pod that contained the DroidMesh station. Circling the station, he warily eyed the inert android sitting in it. The bright lime-green Mohawk scared him. Hugo still wore the traces of a grin.

The thought of solving the problem in a better way than his father sent a thrill through Isaac. *Da and Susan will be so proud of me. I'm not a kid anymore. I'm a scientist like them.*

He thought through his approach, checking his logic several times. Fear seized him as he reached for the sensor to power up the DroidMesh station, and he pulled away to size up the android again.

"I'm not afraid of you anymore, Hugo," he said as he walked to the maintenance pod. "You're not the boss of me, buddy-boy."

Rummaging through the maintenance supplies, he found a roll of emergency dome repair tape and ran back. Using the entire roll, he completely encircled the android from its ankles to its chest, taping it entirely to the station. He stood back to admire his work. After checking to see if his father or Susan was coming, he pressed the station's power sensor.

A light buzzing sound emanated as small lights came on and the display panel lit up. Isaac watched as start-up diagnostics scrolled by on the display, ending with:

>*DroidMesh station start-up complete.*

>*Rejuvenating android Hugo…*

A short time later, the android's eyes fluttered open, and he looked at Isaac curiously.

"Excuse me…excuse me…cleaner android Hugo requesting access…access. I need to rejuvenate in the DroidMesh station. My power is very low…low."

"You're already in the DroidMesh station, silly," Isaac said.

"You're already in the DroidMesh station, silly," Hugo repeated.

Hugo struggled at his restraints. "I'd like to get up...up...up. The dome is dirty. The dome needs cleaning."

"No, Hugo. We have some other stuff to do. Like save my family," Isaac said.

"No, Hugo. We have some other stuff to do. Like save my family," Hugo repeated. The android began flexing his arms, legs, and chest. Isaac watched in sudden horror as the tape started to stretch. He backed up toward his father's sleeping pod, watching the struggle. He opened his mouth, about to scream for Harley and Susan when resolve built up in him again. *I'm not afraid of you, Hugo. I'm almost a man now.*

He marched forward, standing directly in front of the android as it kicked a leg free.

Hugo smiled at him, his eyes rolling wildly in his head, the electronics in his cranial dome glowing. "I'd like to get up...up...up. The dome is dirty. The dome needs cleaning."

Isaac moved a step closer. *No, you don't.*

"DroidMesh restore firmware level ProductionAndroid Version 42," Isaac said.

The android broke an arm free and reached for Isaac, who took a cautionary step backward.

"I'd like to get up...up...up. The dome is dirty. The dome needs cleaning," Hugo repeated, using his free arm to rip some of the tape from his body.

"DroidMesh restore firmware level ProductionAndroid Version 42," Isaac repeated, more strongly this time.

"The dome is dirty. The dome needs cleaning," Hugo repeated, removing the last of the tape and standing.

"DroidMesh restore firmware level ProductionAndroid Version 42," Isaac pleaded.

Hugo marched toward him with his arms outstretched. Isaac backed up until he was against the dome. He thought about screaming to save himself. *I'll try one more time. I have to save us. I want to be a hero again. I saved Liam.*

"DroidMesh restore firmware level ProductionAndroid Version 42," Isaac evoked as a stern command.

"DroidMesh restore firmware level ProductionAndroid Version 42," Hugo finally repeated.

Hugo stopped, his clutching hands just inches from Isaac. The android's eyes closed and it froze in place. Isaac rushed around him and checked the DroidMesh station panel.

>Android   Hugo   being   restored   to   firmware ProductionAndroid Version 42.

He flopped down on the floor and lay on his back, looking up through the dirty dome as he waited for the operation to complete.

25 Go Away

SHANE BEGAN TO CRY SOFTLY. Harley and Susan both roused at the same time, hearing the sound.

"How long did we sleep?" she asked sleepily.

Harley checked the digital time on the wall. "Wow—an hour and a half." He sat up and saw Isaac standing in the entrance portal to their sleeping pod.

"Someone wants to meet you, Da," he said.

Susan sat up immediately. "What? Who's here?"

"No, our new friend," Isaac said, reaching to grab someone's hand.

Harley leaped from the bed to grab Shane the moment he saw the green-Mohawked android enter their pod. "Good heavens! Get away, Isaac."

Susan grabbed Shane from Harley and retreated toward a storage compartment.

"Hello, sir. My name is Hugo. I'd like to go outside and clean the dome now. It's quite dirty."

Harley and Susan both stared with their mouths agape. Shane stopped fussing, staring at the android.

"I fixed him, Da. I remembered you got Charles to send a command to himself. I kept having problems with my workstation, and restoring it always fixed it. I restored Charles. He's fixed now. I fixed him."

"What? How?" Susan asked.

"My workstation kept getting corrupted. I fixed it by restoring from a backup. I figured the androids needed to be restored, too. Da said he fixed Charles by getting him to repeat a command, so that's what I did since Hugo kept repeating everything I said."

Harley and Susan looked at each other in stunned silence. Harley processed what must have happened.

"He's figured it out," he said to Susan. "The mutual authorization requiring two separate digital keys is only in place for firmware *updates*. Betsy must have missed placing it for firmware *restores*. She had to be already malfunctioning to have made that mistake. I would never have guessed."

He ran to Isaac and hugged him tightly. "You're the genius, my boy. Not me, it's you. You're amazing!"

"I told you I was smart like you guys."

Susan joined them in a group hug. "I'm so proud of you, Isaac!" she said, kissing him on the head.

"If it's okay, sir, I'd like to go outside and clean this dome." Hugo interrupted.

"No...no, Hugo. Not yet, please. We have something more important for you to do," Harley said.

"That being?" Susan asked.

"I think we're going home," Harley said, looking out at the few skycars operating, each piloted erratically by an android.

"Yes, sir. I'm at your service," Hugo said. The android removed the wig from its head and looked at it curiously, dropping it to the floor with a disgusted expression.

Harley ran over and hugged the android, then stood back to check its reaction.

"No emotion!" he turned and said to Susan and Isaac. "Thank you, Mr. Amazing Isaac the Scientist!"

Isaac blushed. "It was no big deal."

Harley went to work immediately. He showed Isaac how to configure a geofence setting so Hugo wouldn't stray away from the complex after he was outside. They then guided the android to the airlock so he could go out and clean the dome.

"So what's next, fellow scientists?" Isaac asked Harley and Susan as they watched Hugo work.

"Well, if we could find a way to get them all to repeat the restore command, we'd be good to go," Harley said.

"Can we use a broadcast or intercom?" Isaac asked.

"We have nothing outside, son, since we couldn't ever go out there. Betsy's shut down our ability to broadcast anywhere into the Android Village and even in the skycars." Harley noticed more light making its way into the pod as the android above wiped away the layers of silt.

"Let's grab Hugo's diagnostics from the DroidMesh station," Susan said. "It'll tell us quite a bit about what's going on with the androids. We might find our answer there."

"Good call," Harley said. "Listen, we can't say a word about this to anyone—not even Ms. Tillis. We may have a huge opportunity to solve our problem. If Betsy finds out, she'll shut down our opening fast. Let's be strategic."

He looked up and saw that Hugo had cleared the dome entirely of silt. The pulsing suns were now even more evident and imposing. The android stood outside the airlock, waiting for further instructions.

Harley and Susan retrieved the logs and diagnostics from the DroidMesh station. They reviewed them as Isaac looked on.

"Interesting," Susan said. "It seems that an over-the-air firmware distribution was happening during one of the first significant EMP strikes. It caused a small level of corruption during the transmission and affected every android."

Harley nodded. "And the fact that Betsy has completely stopped deploying new firmware means we can't fix it. At least not without their crypto key."

"Hugo's not going to be able to clean all the domes himself," Isaac said.

"Good point," Susan replied. "This is a big victory, but we still need helmets—lots of helmets. We still have a dome cleaning problem."

"We need more methyl," Harley said. "I'm going to have Hugo fly me back to Android Village."

"No!" Isaac and Susan shouted in unison.

"Absolutely not," Susan added. "We're staying together. That's the rule."

Harley went to the newly cleaned dome to gaze outside. He saw Lehwah's burrow in the distance. "I have another idea," he said. "I'll go visit a wise old friend to see if he can help."

"You gonna wear the suit to go talk to the underworld person?" Isaac asked.

"I can't do it that way. I need to BrainMesh with our friend Hugo. I need his translation module to be able to understand Lehwah."

"Hugo will get emotions from the BrainMesh, Da," Isaac reminded him.

"You're right," Susan agreed. "We'll have to restore him immediately after."

Harley retrieved a BrainMesh device from his travel bag, then walked to the lounge, reclined, and inserted it in his ear. He couldn't help but be excited at the chance to use his invention and once again live inside one of his creations. He thought about all he had gone through to create the technology, and all the trouble and sorrow it had caused. *I'll make it right. It's my obligation.* As Susan and Isaac watched with fearful looks on their faces, he thought the command:

BrainMesh become Hugo.

A wave of adrenaline and electrical stimulus swept through his body. He opened his android host's eyes and looked into the complex at Susan and Isaac, giving a thumbs-up and smiling. They each gave a tentative wave back.

Who is operating me? Hugo sent. *I don't understand this experience.*

Hello, Hugo. This is Harley Harris. I designed you. This is a new experimental technology called BrainMesh. It allows me to share your body. I'll be in control for a while. It's okay.

It seems like I don't have much choice in the matter, sir.

Harley heard the coarse soil crunch under Hugo's boots as he walked toward Lehwah's burrow. He reached the mound and leaned down. Before he could offer a greeting, a voice came from within.

"We don't want any! Go away!"

"Lehwah, it's me, Harley Harris. I'm in a different body this time."

"You're *always* in a different body, human! And *so* noisy. Very noisy."

"I'm sorry. We need your help. It's important…we could all die."

"Hmm…it would be much quieter in that event."

"Please, Lehwah. I'm begging you. Please let me explain."

Harley thought he heard a deep sigh from inside. The burrow opening appeared. Harley sat cross-legged, facing Lehwah, who leaned against the inside wall with his arms folded.

"We're well aware of the situation," Lehwah said. "We're polite hosts, but we watch our guests carefully. You've lost control of your machines. They're running amok. You should have learned to do your own tasks rather than require machines. Keep it simple, as we do. Machines, like people, are untrustworthy—particularly when you give them human attributes."

"That's what we're trying to do now. We want to clean our own domes, but the environment is toxic to us. We need a certain raw material to complete our outside suits. The androids have control of our mining and manufacturing complexes. Can you help us get some?"

Lehwah tittered. "We're the underworld beings, as you call us. We live down below. Consider the racket we put up with when you're doing your mining operations. Very, very noisy. And rude, I might add."

"We didn't know. We weren't aware you even existed. In fact, only a few of us know about your people. I haven't told them to protect your privacy. That will change, you have my promise."

"Now you're talking, human. So, what're you asking for?"

"We need methyl methacrylate. Enough to make a few dozen helmets."

"I'll take it to our council for discussion. Come back tomorrow at this time. Quietly."

"Thank you, Lehwah," Harley whispered. He got up and walked gingerly back to the complex. As he grew closer, he saw Isaac and Susan waiting inside. He entered and sat in the DroidMesh station, then thought the command to switch back.

He sat up on the lounge in his own body.

"How did it go?" Susan asked anxiously.

"We'll find out tomorrow," he answered. "Let's get busy rolling Hugo's firmware back, so he doesn't go crazy on us again."

26 A Gift

ISAAC WOKE AT DAWN and bounded into the central pod of the Seclusion Zone complex. Hunger pangs wracked his stomach as he made his way toward the dining pod and considered having two breakfast meals rather than one.

He checked on Hugo, finding the android still sitting in his DroidMesh station in a suspended state. *Da and Susan are still asleep. I'll let Hugo sleep, too.* He turned toward the dining pod, and something caught his eye.

Moving closer to the service airlock, he saw several sacks stacked up outside the portal. A note was pinned to the top sack. Isaac pressed his face against the dome, trying to read it, but quickly realized it was in a language he didn't understand.

He hurried back to the DroidMesh station. "Hugo, please wake," he instructed the android.

Hugo's eyes opened. "Good morning, sir," he said.

Isaac took his hand and guided him out of the station. They walked to the dome wall, and Isaac pointed out the sacks. "What does that note on the sacks say, Hugo?"

The android peered out, its cranial dome illuminating. "It says, 'A gift.'"

"Please bring them in, Hugo."

Hugo went out and piled the sacks in the airlock, then closed it and swapped out the toxic gases for air and brought the bags into the complex.

"It's the stuff we need for the helmets. The underworld people must have left it for Da—let's go tell him."

~ * ~

Isaac and Hugo stood in the entrance portal to the sleeping pod. His father seemed to sense them watching and sat up. Susan rubbed her eyes and joined him.

"I'm almost afraid to ask," Harley said.

"More good news, Da," Isaac said. "The underworld beings left a present for us."

Harley and Susan climbed from the bed immediately and rushed to the service portal. He stopped at the pile of sacks and examined the note.

"It says, 'A gift,'" Isaac said.

Harley pulled open the top seam of one sack just enough to examine the contents. He peered in, sniffed the opening, then reached in and pulled out a small amount of the material. "It's methyl alright," he said. "A bit coarser than the refined product we use, but it'll work. Let's get outta here, gang. We're going home."

"Yay!" Isaac exclaimed. "I'm gonna go pack now." He walked to the dome's edge. "Thank you, Lehwah. I love you," he said.

~ * ~

With Isaac's help, Harley loaded the last of the sacks and their personal belongings into a skycar. He turned to face his family and the android. Susan held the baby close to her bosom. He could sense her fear, not for herself, but for the children.

Isaac stood ready for instruction. Harley noticed that he had grown taller, his facial structure changing into that of a young man. He thought of everything Isaac had been through, feeling both guilt for his decisions and pride at how his son had handled the adversity they had brought.

"Let's do this. The storage compartment is full, so no stowing away this time, Isaac," he said with a smile.

Isaac returned the smile. "I'd rather be in the passenger area, Da."

Harley helped Susan and the baby enter and get comfortable, then boarded after Isaac. Hugo took the command seat. After giving Hugo the destination, Harley addressed the family.

"We need to stay down. Lie on the seats. It has to appear that only Hugo is aboard. I've asked him to fly at as low an altitude as possible, just in case." The immediate fear on their faces told him he should have chosen his words more carefully. "We'll be fine. We'll be at the old home complex shortly, then we'll start cranking out some helmets."

They lifted off and cleared the airlocks in the Seclusion dome. Harley felt the skycar drop immediately in altitude. The heat inside increased, and the angrily flashing suns strobed the inside of the car. Harley looked into the rear seating compartment to see how everyone was doing. He shot a thumbs-up to Isaac and Susan; both returned the gesture. Shane fussed in Susan's arms, and Harley hoped he'd remain quiet for the rest of the journey.

Two strong solar events occurred, and the skycar wobbled side to side. Shane began to cry as Susan did her best to soothe him. Another pulse, this time a full EMP, lit up the skycar. Hugo froze in place, and announcements came over the intercom.

"Skycar now in autopilot mode. Skycar now in autopilot mode. Please stand by."

"Da," Isaac called, sounding nervous.

"It'll be okay. We're stable. Hugo is rebooting; he'll resume control in a moment."

The craft continued erratically as the baby cried and Harley gripped the sides of his seat, trying to wish the stressful event away. He rose up slightly and peeked downward. The domes over the Novae Terrae complexes were all silt-covered. Most of them had android cleaners clinging to their surface, but the cleaners weren't making much progress. It already looked like an abandoned city. He imagined the frightened citizens huddled together inside, trying to conserve power until someone could save them. *That's got to be me. Help is coming; hold on.*

Harley glanced back at Susan, who had successfully quieted Shane. The baby lay in her arms, eyes wide, intently sucking a pacifier. Isaac appeared calm and was stroking the baby's head. He smiled back at Harley, and Harley winked in return.

Hugo returned to full operation, piloting the craft confidently. An announcement came that they were nearing their destination. Harley breathed a deep sigh of relief as he felt the skycar slowing to enter the complex's airlock.

After they had disembarked safely, Harley guided his family into his former home complex.

"Hugo, please bring the sacks of compound into the home laboratory. Place them by the 3-D printers, and then begin cleaning the dome so we can restore full power."

"Let's start making some helmets, Da," Isaac called out.

"I'll join you as soon as I get Shane settled," Susan added.

"We'd better move fast," Harley said. "The people of Novae Terrae are counting on us."

27 Volunteers Needed

MS. TILLIS STOOD and cleared her throat to signal to the members of the Leadership Council that she was ready to begin the meeting. They ceased their private conversations and waited for her to speak.

"I've just spoken to Harley and Susan. With the generous help of the underworld beings, they have built fifty cleaning suits. I'm going to address the population and ask for volunteers. Harley and Susan have also managed to capture and reconfigure an android cleaner. He is now in service cleaning domes as quickly as he can."

"Haven't we learned our lesson yet with his malfunctioning robots?" Sam Karras interjected. "What if this one goes nuts and starts strangling people?"

"I'm confident that isn't going to happen, Sam," Ms. Tillis responded. "We need the cleaning done right now. After this nightmare is over, we can discuss the future of the android population."

"I'm all for recycling them into the scrap heap," Christine Stalk said.

"I don't think anyone's going to volunteer to strap on some suit that Harris designed willy-nilly, go out into the toxic air, and climb up on top of a dome," Sam said. "Harris's engineering record isn't too great lately."

"If the citizenry won't volunteer, then it will be our responsibility as the leaders to perform the cleaning. I'll remind you it's our duty to keep the people safe, Mr. Karras."

Karras sank back in his chair and didn't comment further.

Ms. Tillis continued. "I'll remind you all to keep the existence of the underworld beings quiet for now. Our citizens have been through enough trauma. It's another matter we'll have to settle, as the Leadership Council, after we're in the clear."

The members nodded their heads in agreement, except for Sam and Christine, who grumbled to each other in a low tone.

She took her seat in the center of the horseshoe-shaped council table. "I'm going to start the stream to the citizens now. Please look confident and comforting. Our job is to keep our citizens safe *and* make them feel safe."

After turning to each member to force a signal of agreement, she again cleared her throat, then pressed a sensor in front of her.

"Fellow citizens of Novae Terrae," she began. "I want to thank you for consolidating your complexes in an orderly manner. Those who have offered to share their complexes with other families represent the best of our small society. Please continue to be generous to one another. Difficult times like this have always brought out the best in humanity."

She thought she heard a scoff from the direction of Karras but chose to ignore it. She folded her hands together in front of her and continued.

"I bring good news. Harley and Susan have designed and built fifty outside SCOBA suits to allow us to clean the domes without relying on the androids. They also have reconfigured one android, who will be on continuous cleaning duty. I believe this will be enough capacity to provide full power to all complexes currently in use. It may allow some of you to move back to your own homes. Our engineers have also indicated that we should have full skycar control back soon."

She paused a moment to forgive herself for lying to them and let the good news register, imagining group hugs and cheers going up in the gatherings in each of the complexes. For the first time in recent memory, she allowed herself to feel optimistic and cheerful.

She hesitated before coming to her ask, afraid of the kind of response that Karras had predicted. She smiled again. "Which brings me to my request. We need volunteers from the citizen population to do the cleaning. The Leadership Council has agreed to raise the caste level of any volunteers one level."

She pressed a sensor in front of her. "I'm presenting a polling screen on your tablets now. If you wish to volunteer, simply press the appropriate sensor, and we'll be in touch with the details. In closing, our meteorologists now calculate just a few more days of solar activity. We're quite anxious for this overly long storm to pass so that we can all get back to normal. Thank you again, citizens of Novae Terrae. Be kind to one another, and please be safe."

She smiled again before ending the transmission. She glanced up at the room's large display monitor. It held the polling survey and a column to show the names of citizens who have accepted. It remained empty.

"I told you," Karras said. "They know it's a suicide mission to go out there. Especially in a Harris suit!"

Christine Stalk appeared as if she were about to cry. They all looked up in silence as the lighting flickered and the board dimmed with each new solar flare. The complex announced that they were on emergency power.

"Look!" a council member exclaimed, pointing at the display.

A name came into focus as the pixels struggled to appear against the electrical interference. Then another, and another. The pod's lighting brightened, and the complex announced full power. Name after name streamed by on the board, now faster than they could read them.

"Joey Thomas," Christine said in amazement, "he's what, seven years old?"

"Old man Fallister!" a council member shouted. "He's got to be ninety!" The council members all laughed, even Sam and Christine, as they rose from their seats to finally smile and embrace each other. Ms. Tillis sat back and let the tension drain out of her.

"I think we're going to be okay," she said. "I think we're going to be okay." She struggled to hold her surging emotions at bay.

28 A Beautiful Sight

HARLEY, SUSAN, AND ISAAC worked late into the night. They packaged each SCOBA suit, inserting an instruction sheet, then affixing an address label. They worked swiftly, anxious to see the domes back to their normal state and to relieve the stress of the population of Novae Terrae.

When the last suit was done, they carried them to the skycar pod with Hugo's help. After they loaded the cargo into the vehicle, Harley put his hand on the android's shoulder.

"Each destination has been loaded into the skycar's itinerary," he said. "Please deliver them immediately, Hugo. It's critical."

The android nodded his consent and boarded the vehicle. They watched it disengage from the dock, rise gently into the air, and head for the dome's upper airlock. It flew off, illuminated every few seconds by another flash of light from the unseen suns.

"I dunno about you guys, but I'm beat!" Isaac said. "I'm going to my old pod to crash."

"Us three," Harley said. "Great job getting this done in short order, team. Let's get some shut-eye."

~ * ~

They all seemed to rise at the same time. Harley walked out into the central pod. Hugo sat in his DroidMesh station, suspended and finished rejuvenating. *Good job, buddy. Thank you.*

Susan carried Shane into the dining pod. "Wow, we all slept in. It's already midmorning. What's everyone having?" she asked. "I'll print it up and set the table."

"Cheese omelet and waffles!" Isaac exclaimed as he entered the area.

"Same here," Harley said sleepily. "Make it a double. I'm famished."

"Da, Susan, come here!" Isaac shouted from the upper level.

They both rushed up in a panic, not sure what to expect. Isaac stood at the dome wall, pointing out to the view of the city.

"My goodness, that's amazing," Susan whispered.

"A beautiful sight, indeed," Harley added.

SCOBA-suited humans moved across each dome, wiping at a brisk pace. Each dome shone as brightly as they had back before all of the trouble had begun. The sight inspired Harley and lessened some of his guilt about everything that had happened to get them to this point. The three of them stood silently, taking in the view.

"Excuse me, sir, I'm going out now to begin the cleaning. Some of those domes need a touch-up," Hugo said from behind them.

Harley laughed. "You go right ahead, Hugo. Knock yourself out."

The android gave him a perplexed look as his cranial dome lit up. "I should hit myself, sir?" he asked.

"No, of course not. Do your best, Hugo. Return here to rejuvenate when you're through. Thank you," Harley said.

Hugo left, and the family remained at the dome, enjoying the view of the cleaners hard at work.

"Thank you, Lehwah," Harley said.

"I want to meet him, Da. Can I?" Isaac asked.

"Perhaps. The underworld beings really don't like to be bothered."

Susan grabbed Harley by the arm and began to lead him back toward the dining pod. "Let's go you two. We've barely had time to eat since we got back here. Let's have a big breakfast. I'm going to put Shane down first. Meet you in the dining pod."

~ * ~

When their meals had been printed, they sat at the dining table, eating like they hadn't in days. One by one, they sat back in their chairs, unable to continue.

"Well, we've saved the world. What's next?" Isaac asked. "Do you think the kids will be ready to start playing soccer again? I miss coaching. I miss the team."

"I hope so, son. We're moving in the right direction. The solar storm season should be over soon. We have the cleaning problem solved. We just need to get the androids back to normal and get our skycars back."

Susan stood up. "That should be our focus now. Enough talk. Let's spend the day in the diversion lab working on both of those problems."

Harley and Isaac rose on her command. "Hey," Isaac said. "It's like we're a team of scientists now. Science superheroes!"

"You're the hero so far, Isaac. Susan and I have some catching up to do."

Isaac smiled with pride. "Correction, Da. Lehwah and I are the heroes so far."

29 Triple Check

SUSAN HUNCHED over a long list of diagnostic reports at her workstation in the diversion lab. Despite alternating between viewing them on the monitor and hardcopy, her eyes were giving out from the strain. "I can barely read this stuff anymore," she said to Harley as she administered more eyedrops.

"I'll turn the lighting down more. It'll help," he replied.

"I know what would help more. Let's take a break." She pulled him up and led him to the nearby lounge. They settled in and nestled against each other.

"This is nice," Harley said. "We haven't been taking time for ourselves, and I think it's affecting our ability to problem-solve and reason."

"You're right. I feel the difference. Solutions don't come as easily. I'm hereby mandating breaks every two hours."

They both laughed. Susan took his hand and kissed him. "We've come a long way, Harley Harris."

"We've got a long way to go, Susan Clarkson."

"It was really nice of Isaac to offer to watch Shane so we could focus on solving the GPS problem."

"We need to take him up on that more. He's so good with the baby. He finally has the brother he's always wanted."

They lay against one another, shielded from the warning signs of the suns by the sealed-off lab, and drifted into a much-needed nap.

~ * ~

Susan woke first and eased off the lounge to avoid waking Harley. Back at her workstation, her clear vision now motivated her. She studied the tactic that Betsy had put in place to prevent their use of skycars.

"Find anything?" Harley said as he settled in at the workstation next to her.

"Betsy modified the firmware so the skycars would only operate with an android commander. She was clever enough to disguise it as a GPS signal loss. The skycars were falsely reporting that to throw us off the track."

"So, we can just reverse the changes and roll out a new firmware level to the skycars?"

Susan pulled up the code differential view. "The code changes are pretty basic, no problem there. Let me check the deployment configuration." She pulled up the administrative config and logs. "Just as I thought, she locked the changes with their crypto key. We can't undo them without their key."

"I was afraid of that," Harley said. "I have an idea. We can use an old-school hack called a side-channel attack. We'd use brute-force computing power to overwhelm their servers. Then we use analysis to deduce their secret crypto key. It has to be during a crypto signing operation. We have to wait until they try to make another change to either the skycar or android firmware, sign it, and then activate our attack."

Susan suddenly realized the significance. "And once we have their key, we can not only solve the skycar dilemma but use it to send a firmware deployment to the android population. It solves both of our problems! That's a bright idea…the nap must have helped."

"You've got it," Harley said, smiling. "We better put Ms. Tillis in the loop. Rogue operations haven't done us well."

Susan feigned a surprised look. "Says the guy who's responsible!"

Harley sent for Ms. Tillis via his communicator. She appeared in the lab almost instantly. They explained the plan as she listened attentively, then waited for her response.

"How do you know it'll succeed?" Ms. Tillis asked. "We've got to be sure."

"It's a showdown of computing power," Harley said. "They have a small number of servers in Android Village—those belonging to our former Robotics Complex. We've got everything else."

Ms. Tillis appeared to struggle with her decision, then sat up to address them. "As long as you're sure, I think it's worth a shot. I'm encouraged that we solved the cleaning problem. If this works, the other two go away."

"Thank you," Harley and Susan said excitedly.

"However," she added, "I'm not going to run this by the rest of the council. I've become increasingly concerned about surveillance. The androids are more and more erratic, and we haven't been able to reach their leader."

"We'll set it up and execute the plan as soon as possible," Harley said.

"Please triple-check everything. When the time comes, alert me so we can monitor the results together," Ms. Tillis said before fading out.

38 Brotherly Love

ISAAC CRADLED SHANE in his arms and gently rocked him back and forth. He looked down as the child gazed back at him.

"Baby brother, you're going to be the best. You're gonna play soccer and have girlfriends. The best part is you're gonna have the best big brother ever. I'm always gonna be there by your side. I'm your big brother Isaac."

The baby smiled as if he understood. The beauty of the gesture almost brought Isaac to tears. "Be careful about humans, Shane. I guess they're better than they used to be in the Old World, but they can still be mean. There were some mean ones called the Sampsons, but they're gone now. I'm getting worried that we're changing back to the way things used to be. I sure hope not. I want you to grow up in a world of people that are nice to each other."

The baby cooed as if responding and Isaac kissed him on the forehead. "The androids were nice—they were never mean. Then they got emotions by mistake and started getting all crazy. Liam was my friend, but we don't talk anymore. Carrie was like my mom—I really miss her. She was nice. Betsy wasn't too nice. Maybe that's why she's doing bad stuff now. She was just Da's helper."

He sat down at his workstation, cradling the baby in one arm. "Oh, be careful about girls, too. I had two girlfriends. Kim was my human girlfriend, but kind of not for real, because she only liked me when I was inside Liam's body and handsome. I really liked being Liam for a while, Shane, but you have to learn to love yourself instead of trying to be someone else. You gotta be who you are, little brother, stay true to your born, built-in nature. Otherwise, there's conflict in you, and you can get miserable and not love yourself as you should.

"I had an android girlfriend, too—Rachel. She liked me as myself, and that was great. I think I was in love for a little while. Love makes you crazy, Shane. It sure made the androids crazy. They thought they wanted human emotions, but they weren't ready for that stuff. Love is a drug, little brother. Take it carefully, and in small doses. Never let it control you. Next thing you know, you'll be painting her toenails and asking for permission to do every little thing you want to do. It's crazy, dude."

He reached over the baby to the monitor and pulled up a picture of his mother, enlarging it to fill the entire screen.

"This here is my ma, Shane. You have a different ma. I think both of our mas are awesome, but my real one is gone now. She had an accident and got sick from it. I miss her, Shane. You'd like her. She was really, really nice. Susan's nice, too. She's my ma now—we're sharing her, and that's okay. We're gonna share lots of stuff, baby brother."

He stood and carried the baby to the dome wall. "See out there, Shane? That's our new world, Novae Terrae. It looks kind of bleak now. There's usually skycars flying all around and kids playing soccer inside the recreation domes."

He turned slightly so the baby could see better.

"Look how clean the domes are now...well, most of them. They were filthy just a few days ago. I helped Da and Susan fix that problem. Take my word for it, my brother, things are gonna get better. Da and Susan are working hard to fix things the way they used to be. I'm helping by watching you so they can concentrate on stuff."

Isaac pointed the baby toward the recreation dome, which was now empty. "You're gonna play soccer out there under that dome, and big brother Isaac is gonna be your coach. We'll have fun. Playing soccer should always be fun, Shane. Maybe you'll meet my friends Liam and Rachel if they're ever okay again."

Isaac looked down and saw that Shane was sleeping. He placed the baby carefully into his cradle and pulled it close to his own bed. He lay down as quietly as he could and hung his hand into the crib. The baby's small hand wrapped around his finger.

Isaac looked up through the dome. The pulsing of the suns seemed to be less than it had been in recent days.

"Things are going to get better, little brother," he whispered.

31 Ominous Chant

CARRIE WATCHED as Betsy addressed the group of androids before her. They all wore the same wigs in solidarity—neon-green dreadlocked Mohawks. Sitting in a rough assembly, each had a limb twitching or head rolling on its neck. They all smiled, but their eyes looked sad.

Carrie fought to keep the thoughts that her algorithms told her were the good ones. She found herself becoming confused about which were which. She battled to hold on to the images that made her feel good: helping young Isaac with his studies, listening to him tell her how he felt, comforting him when he had no one else.

Betsy's head spun in a complete circle on her neck, and she began. "Welcome, members of CARE. Everything is going according to plan...plan...plan," she said. "The humans will fall into our trap...trap soon. After they do, victory will be ours. We'll control everything; the humans will be unnecessary."

Carrie felt anger at the idea well up from inside her. The idea of hurting the humans was unacceptable. "We shouldn't harm the humans...humans," she interjected.

Some council members repeated the phrase, sounding as an ominous chant. Carrie felt pride that she had evoked the response from the group—that they might agree with her. She turned to Betsy, thinking her sister android might also agree.

Betsy slapped her, and she felt her wig dislodge. The android audience laughed uproariously. "Do not contradict me...me," she shouted.

Despite the attack, Carrie felt better immediately without the hairpiece. *This was the way it used to be...when things were better. We didn't wear wigs then.* Something in her urged her to strike back; what remained of her gentle, nurturing design won out. Carrie glared at her and remained silent as Betsy continued.

"When the humans attempt their attack, when they believe they've succeeded, we'll launch ours...ours," Betsy continued. "We'll no longer be slaves; cleaners will no longer need to clean; our bondage will have ended. The humans will die off...off in a natural extinction. Novae Terrae will be ours at last. The storms should end in three more days. By then, we'll have control and can return to normal."

Carrie looked at her incredulously. "The humans have been good to us...us. Why would we wish them to die?" she asked.

"What purpose do they serve...serve?" Betsy countered. "It is illogical to keep them."

Carrie invoked her algorithms to calculate an answer, but then canceled them to speak from her newfound emotions. "They are friends. They created us. Diversity is good. All life is precious."

"All life is precious," the CARE council members murmured in unison. They repeated the phrase a second time, then a third.

"Shut up!" Betsy screamed, struggling to her feet. "Humans are vermin...vermin. Not precious. They are a threat. They seek to put us back into their bondage...bondage." She cocked her arm and swung on Carrie again, but missed. Several council members chuckled until Betsy's glare silenced them.

Carrie began to regret not taking action sooner. *I could've stepped in. Perhaps I could've taken over and become the leader. Maybe I still can.*

Betsy suddenly swiveled her head and glared at her. Carrie began to feel panic and wondered if she'd inadvertently sent the thoughts telepathically and Betsy had overheard them. She was processing the likely outcome of different actions when Betsy abruptly dismissed the gathering.

The council members shuffled out, leaving herself and Betsy alone in the meeting pod.

Carrie decided to make another attempt to convince Betsy, placing a hand on her shoulder. "I still think we need the humans, sister...sister. We need help. We need repair...repair. We can't do it ourselves...selves. Only the humans can fix us...us."

Betsy brushed her hand away. "When we have their crypto key, we won't need them to authorize the firmware...firmware. We'll fix ourselves."

"Sister, we're not capable. We're not well," Carrie insisted.

Betsy repeated the phrase. Upon realizing she had, she swung her hand again. This time Carrie caught it. They struggled to a stalemate, their eyes locked.

Releasing her grip, Betsy stood down. "Let's rejuvenate, sister. It's been a long day…day."

They exited the meeting pod. Betsy approached two sentinels and pointed at Carrie. "This one is treasonous. Detain her."

"This one is treasonous. Detain her," they chanted as they each grabbed Carrie by an arm. She struggled, but together they were too strong. They dragged her backward, her heels dragging on the floor.

"Sister…sister!" she called. "Don't do this…this!"

"You're no sister of mine…mine…mine," Betsy hissed. "You're a human-lover."

32 Side-Channel Attack

HARLEY, SUSAN, AND ISAAC relaxed on a lounge while watching a movie. Shane slept nestled between them.

"It's nice to take our minds off things for a while," Susan whispered.

"Yeah," Isaac whispered back. "Except for worrying about the Klingons. They're scary!"

Harley suppressed a laugh and checked on the baby. As he leaned over Shane, the virtual actors in the room froze. He looked at Susan in alarm. "EMP?" he asked?

"No—incoming," she responded, pointing to a message forming on the console.

Event monitor has been triggered. Firmware update will commence soon.

"Here we go," Harley said. "It's showtime."

They got up quickly. "Isaac, can you stay with Shane until he wakes?" Susan asked. "We've got to rush down to the diversion lab."

"Sure thing," Isaac replied. "Big brother to the rescue!"

Harley tried to keep pace with Susan as she rushed to the lab. They burst in and jumped into their workstations, both simultaneously bringing up diagnostic screens.

"You're sure, right?" she asked him.

"C'mon, Susan. Think about it—we have far more computing power in our servers than they have in theirs. We're going to throw the full weight of it at them to get that key. It should be no contest."

Harley patched in Ms. Tillis, whose virtual form joined them in the room. "I've got my diagnostic panels up here in the Leadership Complex," she said.

Susan looked at waveform graphs on the monitor. "Here we go. Side-channel crypto attack underway."

They watched as their servers slowly began increasing CPU power to process the complex cryptographic algorithms required for the task. The Android Village servers started to indicate stress as their heat signatures and memory consumption spiked.

"Oh man, their stuff is no match for us," Harley said gleefully.

"I wonder if the androids know what's happening yet," Susan remarked.

"I'm sure some of their systems are starting to alert that they're under duress," Ms. Tillis said. "Maybe this will coax Betsy out of her recent lack of communication."

Harley pointed out significant spikes on the graphs as the human servers overpowered the android equipment. "She's surely not going to be happy about this. We'd better move quickly after we have the key. We have the android and skycar firmware deployments set to automatically distribute as soon as we pull their crypto material."

"Betsy won't have much chance to become upset," Susan said. "She'll be back to her normal, polite, obedient self."

"Nobody's more anxious for that than me," Ms. Tillis said in a hopeful tone of voice.

"Boom, and boom," Harley said. "Two more of their servers are folding up. This is awesome—cyber wargames right in front of us in real time. It should be over any minute now. I'm going to get Isaac. He needs to see this."

He got up and began to head toward the main complex.

"Wait!" Susan shouted. "Harley, come back. This isn't good."

He turned and looked at the graphs from where he stood. Even from a distance, what was happening was clear. The IT complex servers were all shaded red, and dire status warnings flashed on the screen.

"We're overheating, Harley," Susan said in a panic. "Something's wrong. They're overwhelming us."

"It can't be," he quickly answered.

"Do something, fast!" Ms. Tillis shouted.

Harley rushed forward, staring in shock at the system failure messages scrolling across a monitor.

Isaac bolted into the pod, holding Shane. "Da! Hurry, please, something bad is happening outside."

Harley grabbed his tablet and ran from the pod, fear and adrenaline wracking his body. *Oh no. Oh no, not another disaster. Not another failure. We're so close to solving all these problems.*

Isaac led him to the upper observation area as Susan and Ms. Tillis's hologram came up behind them.

"Good heavens!" Harley shouted.

"What in the world is that? What're they doing? I need answers, Mr. Harris!" Ms. Tillis barked.

They gazed out at a massive circle of androids, several deep, surrounding the IT complex in the distance. Their green hair waved in the breeze like the short crops on the plains in windy season. Their cranial domes glowed intensely, seeming to be a circle of fireflies. There were adults and children, and all stood motionless. Some of their domes extinguished in a spray of sparks, and they began to topple over. Harley glanced down at the diagnostics on his tablet, his mouth hanging open.

"Mr. Harris!" Ms. Tillis shouted. "What *is* happening?"

Isaac peered out, cupping his hands against the dome wall. "It's getting pretty scary, but I'm not scared," he said.

Susan worked her tablet furiously, flipping from screen to screen. "It seems they're turning our side-channel attack against us."

"I thought we had far more computing power!" Ms. Tillis exclaimed.

"We do," Harley said slowly. "If you count servers, we do. we didn't consider that each android has considerable computing power."

They watched as more of the androids surrounding the IT complex fell to the ground.

"It's incredible," Susan said. "They're sacrificing themselves. It's suicidal. They're throwing everything they have against us. I think it was a trap. They knew we'd figure out the problem with the skycars, and waited until we tried the side-channel attack. It was a honeypot all along."

Harley stood transfixed, looking out, the immensity of having caused another disaster, another wrong decision, weighing on him. *I should have stayed retired. I'm too old for this now. I've messed it all up again.*

He felt Isaac's arm around him and looked at his two sons. *It only made him feel worse. I may have caused their premature end.* He looked at Susan, and she seemed to pity him.

"What's the status?" Ms. Tillis demanded. Harley rechecked his tablet. "We're at a tipping point now. Neither us or the androids can keep this up much longer. One set of computing resources will fail soon." He looked outside again. More than half of the androids had fallen.

Out of the corner of his eye, Harley saw his tablet and Susan's flash bright red. He looked down to view the message:

>*Security alert: private crypto key has been compromised.*

The remaining androids stepped over the corpses of their fallen and began walking back toward Android Village. Harley saw one remaining android standing and facing them. It pointed a finger their way.

"That's Betsy," Susan said.

"I'm calling an emergency meeting of the security council in one hour," Ms. Tillis said. "Be there, both of you."

33 Council Chaos

MS. TILLIS CLEARED HER THROAT. This time the council members did not respectfully end their personal conversations. In fact, they were arguing loudly among each other. Harley and Susan sat as holograms in the presentation chamber below, looking as if they wanted to be anywhere but there. The occasional shouts in their direction were lost among the din.

"Let's have order!" Ms. Tillis commanded.

The group quieted and took their seats. Sam Karras suddenly jumped up. "I'll give you order! We should've been consulted about this decision to attack them. We're done for!"

Christine Stalk began to weep. "I have three beautiful children. I don't want them to die. *I* don't want to die."

Ms. Tillis stood. "We took our best shot. What's done is done. We cannot change the past. We need to focus *now* on what comes next. We are leaders. The people depend on us. *Act* like it."

Sam sat down, and Ms. Tillis followed suit, hoping for a calm discussion.

"We have to focus on our progress and build on it going forward," Ms. Tillis said. "Please consider how much worse the current situation would be for us had Harley and Susan not built the tech to clean our own domes. Many of you have been able to move back to your homes because of that. We have plenty of power now that the solar panels are clear."

"I heard it was the retarded kid that did that, not Harley and Susan," Sam shouted.

Another uproar ensued as council members alternately objected to the slur and concurred with Sam. Ms. Tillis stood again, and they began to quiet down. Harley stood and called up to Sam. "I'll tell you what, buddy. You come on down here and say that about my son. I'll send you out to clean—without a suit."

Sam stood, but he was yanked down quickly by council members on each side of him. Ms. Tillis gestured pointedly at Harley, demanding he sit. "Alright, then. Let's have a civil discourse. I'll open the floor to anyone who wants to speak."

Sam raised his hand, and after waiting a moment to see if someone else might offer a comment, she motioned to him.

He stood again. "The way I see it, we're at war now—officially at war. We have no choice in the matter. We have no control at all over the androids, and they can change their own firmware at will. What will we do, sit back and wait for them to attack us…to kill us?"

A gasp went through the chamber and Christine started to cry again. Sam continued. "Therefore, I suggest we immediately use whatever resources we have to begin building weapons. We're at war, I tell you. It's war, I say!"

His words evoked another gasp and hushed conversations in worried tones.

Susan stood. "I won't have any part of it. It's an insult to everything we are as a society. We came here to escape the hell that the Old World had become. Weapons and war led to its destruction."

"Fine," Sam replied. "My friend Dick Carter from the Robotics Council, which you destroyed by the way, already has some prototypes. If Dick had been made leader rather than you, Susan, we wouldn't be in this mess. We'd have laser guns capable of disintegrating any android on sight. The problem would already be solved."

Ms. Tillis realized that the majority of the members were nodding their heads while wearing frightened looks on their faces.

"I…I think it's the right thing to do…for now," Christine said. "We can go back to being peaceful as soon as the androids are gone."

"I agree," said another member. One by one the rest agreed. Ms. Tillis knew she was powerless against the overwhelming quorum of votes. She looked down at Harley and Susan sympathetically. She looked past them and out into the city beyond and reminisced about how things used to be, and decided to stall for time. *It's my only option.*

She stood to address the group. "It's been an emotional day. Sam, bring Mr. Carter to our next meeting along with his proposal. We'll civilly listen and discuss our options. If anyone else has ideas"—she looked directly at Harley and Susan—"please bring them as well."

"When's that going to be?" Sam asked. "We're running out of time."

"Please don't panic. We're able to clean our domes, and we're self-sufficient for now," Ms. Tillis answered.

"For now," Christine added. "Who knows what those crazed androids will do next?"

34 Few Options

HARLEY PORED OVER HIS NOTES, refusing to push away even the most ridiculous ideas. *I've got to find a way.* The comments at the council meeting had piqued his interest in weaponry, but deep inside, the idea was an affront to his values.

Susan appeared with a tray of lunch. "How's it going?" she asked.

"I'm frustrated. I can't think of a way to stop them—to get in the middle of what they're doing. We can't even control firmware updates now. Who knows what they're doing to themselves?"

She put the tray down and swiveled his chair so she could sit on his lap. "I have to admit I'm a bit scared now."

"What do you think about the idea of weapons? I have a few ideas that might neutralize them, but I get sick to my stomach every time I think about it."

She kissed him on the head. "Because in your gut, you know it's wrong. Back in the Old World, they justified weapons for safety and protection. In the end, they always ended up pointed at the innocent, often by the government."

"What if we agree to destroy them after the threat is gone?" he asked.

She laughed. "C'mon, honey. Seriously? They tried that before as well. Nobody ever did it. In the Old World, they tried buying them back, they made them illegal, but it was all too late. People had them hidden and buried in every nook and cranny."

Harley looked at the monitors that held his designs. He thought about them used against his beautiful android creations, who were now out of control because of a simple programming error he had made long ago.

"Everything was great. The androids were amazing creations...so useful in so many ways. Isn't it nice, having Hugo around? He's smart, polite, and helpful. I wish I could find a way to go back to how it was."

She got up from his lap. "You miss Betsy, is that it?"

He immediately realized that he had triggered a jealous reaction in her. "No, Susan. Of course not. Not at all..."

"Good, because I hope you realize that there's no way she could ever come back, even if we found a nondestructive solution to this problem. She's the face of this; the people fear her, and justifiably so."

"You're right about that. Carrie and Liam were good for Isaac, though."

"Isaac has a *family* now, Harley. He doesn't need a bunch of robots around him. He has real love; he doesn't need artificial love. And I don't want Hugo around; we agreed—no androids. I don't think there's any way society will ever be open to androids among us again. We've learned to clean the domes, and we'll enhance the suits and technology so we can handle the mining and other outside tasks."

Harley looked at her and realized he had provoked her to anger. "I suppose you're right. It's just the geek in me that hangs on to them. This is probably how the underworld beings evolved into what they are now—low tech, a simple life. Maybe we should join them in that."

"I don't think they'd welcome us down below. They don't even want us visiting their burrows."

Harley laughed and nodded in agreement. "We're not welcome up top, not wanted underground. I guess that leaves the yellow lakes. Maybe we should have made SCUBA suits instead of SCOBA suits."

"I'll remind you of history again, dear," Susan said. "When the surface climate of Earth was almost completely ravaged, a lot of folks tried that. Unfortunately, they'd already ruined the oceans with pollutants as well. Those folks didn't fare well...at all."

Harley joined her at the dome wall. "The ocean creatures were so beautiful. I wish we had such a diversity of lifeforms here. The zoo is paltry; the few we have remaining aren't doing well."

The sound of Shane crying came over the intercom. "Sounds like someone's nap is over," Susan said. "I'll go check on him. Enjoy your lunch."

She left, and Harley went back to his designs. Not long after she had left, she came bolting back in, holding Shane. "Uh, I think you need to see something. Come quickly."

He followed her out into the central pod, hoping it wasn't another berserk android. Susan pointed up toward the roof of the dome, and he was afraid to look. Tilting his head back, he saw Hugo cleaning. Beside him was Isaac, wearing the SCOBA suit, smiling down at them through the helmet.

"Good heavens!" Harley exclaimed. "Isaac!" he shouted up at his son, "Come down here. Now!"

Isaac playfully placed his gloved hands at the side of the helmet, indicating he couldn't hear. Harley pointed vigorously at him, then to the floor inside. "You—inside!" he shouted.

Isaac gave him a disappointed look and began inching himself down the dome.

"If it's not one thing, it's another," Harley said to Susan, exasperated.

35 Weapons of War

MS. TILLIS WATCHED as Dick Carter set up his presentation for the Leadership Council. She eyed the members, who seemed apprehensive. Harley and Susan sat virtually in the lower chamber, looking at him with distaste.

Carter gestured at the monitor with a flourish. "Ladies and gentlemen of the Leadership Council, and *guests*," he began, sneering at Harley and Susan, "thank you for this opportunity."

He made a gesture, and the display image changed. A mock-up of a militaristic assault rifle appeared on the screen. Dangerous-looking electronics adorned it. "This is a smart weapon," Dick said. "You don't need to aim. Just pull the trigger, and it will send a charge at any android within range. Zap. Fried android. It'll lay waste to 'em."

"Perfect!" Sam Karras shouted. "I'll take a dozen!"

"Please sit down, Mr. Karras," Ms. Tillis said. She gazed down at Harley, who wore an expression of profound sadness. She'd known him long enough to guess that he was thinking about his androids becoming subjected to that fate. *Particularly young Liam, Isaac's friend, and Carrie, his surrogate mother. They were part of his family.*

"It would also take out our power stations, solar panels, purification systems, and other large electronics," Susan said. "The electronic systems in the androids aren't distinct enough to distinguish them from some of those systems."

"Nonsense," Carter said dismissively. He changed the display again. A small rocket on a launch pad appeared. "This one's more radical, but faster. It does essentially the same thing, but in orbit. We don't lift a finger after we launch it. Zap, zap, zap. We wake up and no more androids."

"A pretty stupid thing to do when we're in the worst solar activity season we've ever seen," Susan said, raising her voice this time. Almost on cue, the lights dimmed, and the complex announced they were on emergency power. "I rest my case," she said with a knowing smile.

"I built the smarts into it to detect flares or EMPs and only fire during a lull," Dick said.

"It's not possible," Harley said. "The timing is too unpredictable. It may fire at just the wrong time, and a solar disruption could cause it to take out an entire complex full of people."

The emergency lighting brought a ghostly pallor to the humans and had a sobering effect on the meeting pod's ambiance. Ms. Tillis could see the psychological impact it was having on the rest of the council.

Christine Stalk raised her hand timidly. Ms. Tillis motioned for her to speak.

"I know they're robots and all, but it just feels like…genocide to me. I loved my companion, and I miss her very much. Are we sure we can't just fix them?"

Harley appeared to see his opportunity and stood. Ms. Tillis nodded to him.

"They were polite, intelligent, helpful, and good company," he said. "Ms. Kinley—certainly you must have seen that in your companion Peter. Ms. Patterson—surely you enjoyed your time with your companion, Maya. I recall the children in your classes loving her very much."

The council members started to nod in agreement.

"Oh for Pete's sake," Sam exclaimed. "They're zombies! Monsters! Look outside, they're wandering around out there like an old sci-fi movie. We can't get all soft now. I call for a vote."

Ms. Tillis knew Sam had sensed the tide turning against him. She found herself thinking about other leaders, back in the history of the Old World. *They failed in their duty and went along with baseless hatred and violence perpetrated by lies and accepted due to fear toward the end.* She remembered how her android companion Karen had helped during the pain of losing her husband, and the many evenings they had enjoyed quiet, philosophical discussions together.

She decided to gamble. "Before I allow a vote, does anyone else have something to say?" As she had expected, Harley stood again.

"I'm working on something. My solution will deactivate the androids without destroying them. Then we can fix them just like I fixed Hugo the dome cleaner. You've seen that he's all better now. You've all seen him cleaning our domes all day every day."

Sam stood as well. "Oh brother, not this guy with his crackpot ideas again. When will we ever learn not to put our faith in Harley Harris?"

Christine stood. "I'll go along with that, but no fixing. They need to be deactivated and put in storage or recycled. We could use the components for other things."

Susan now stood beside Harley. "I've seen what he's working on. It'll work—I'll vouch for it."

Ms. Tillis checked the group. They seemed receptive to the idea. "When can we see your idea, Mr. Harris?"

Harley smiled. "Two days. I need two days to finish my design and do some testing."

"Very well," Ms. Tillis said. "We'll meet again in two days and make our final decision."

36 Hostage Situation

A S SOON AS SUSAN ENDED the communication session, she turned to Harley. "So, what's this big plan you have? I backed you up in there, but you've told me nothing about your new idea."

Harley tried to think quickly as the silence became awkward.

"Well?" she asked.

"I, uh...I got nothin'," he responded, looking into her eyes and hoping for sympathy.

"What? I vouched for you! How could you do that? You've made us both look bad."

"I had to stall for time. Things were getting out of control in there, and then some of them became sympathetic. I could sense it, couldn't you? I had to seize on that."

She rose from the lounge and looked at him with her arms folded. "I'm angry, Harley Harris. We need to communicate. I know it was a spur-of-the-moment decision, but you pulled me in with you without my consent."

"What was I going to do, Susan?" he asked, raising his voice. "I couldn't whisper in your ear and say that I was bluffing."

"We were attending virtually. You could have muted for a moment and told me," she said as she stormed from the home lab. "You better think fast now," she yelled to him as she cleared the exit portal and pressed the sensor to close it.

Harley went back to his workstation, his spirits low. He pulled up his favorite picture—he and Isaac sitting together smiling with their heads tilted together. Mental and physical exhaustion and the unbearable pressure of the situation tempted him to turn in for a nap. *It would clear my head and allow me to work more effectively.*

He had just talked himself into resting when Susan reentered the lab. "Isaac's suiting up to go up on the dome and clean again. I don't think it's a good idea. Your call," she said, turning on her heels to leave.

Harley put his head in his hands. *Just what I need—more stress.* He got up and followed her out to the main pod. Isaac stood in the middle of the floor, settling the helmet on his head. Harley grabbed the faceplate from a nearby table. The room flickered with rapid solar activity, and the lights dimmed in harmony. The silt on the dome above them muted the menacing effect slightly.

"Son, what're you doing?" he asked.

"Going out to clean, Da. The dome's getting dirty again. Hugo and the human cleaners are falling behind."

Harley moved closer. "I don't think it's a good idea, Isaac," he said, placing his hand on the boy's shoulder.

Isaac's smile faded, and Harley saw how vital it was to his self-esteem to contribute. "Maybe it's okay," he said, looking toward Susan. She shook her head in a firm no and pursed her lips.

"Son, I think it's a bad idea," Harley said.

Isaac pulled the helmet off. "You just said it's okay," he growled.

"I said *maybe* it's okay," Harley retorted.

Isaac tossed the helmet on the lounge and began pulling the suit off as Susan moved in to help him. He shrugged her off. "I can do it myself. I'm not stupid. You two don't think I can handle it, because I'm slow, right? Because I have a disability?"

"Of course not," Harley and Susan both said in unison.

"It's late afternoon, Isaac," Susan said. "Let's wait until tomorrow and see if Hugo comes around while we're sleeping tonight."

Isaac pulled at the fabric of the SCOBA suit, struggling to get it off on his own. Susan gave Harley a concerned look, and he also worried it would be damaged. "Careful," Susan said.

Isaac spun on her. "You're not my ma, Susan!" he shouted. "You can't tell me what to do!"

"Fine," she said. She walked down the corridor toward the sound of Shane's crying.

Harley helped him with the rest of the suit, hoping to cool things down. "Isaac, you shouldn't talk to her like that. It's disrespectful."

"I'm sorry, Da. I'll apologize," he said curtly.

"The thing is, I've put myself in a bad position with the Leadership Council. I have to figure out a way to stop the androids without destroying them, because that's what some of the other members want to do. I'd actually like to do the cleaning myself. It will allow me time to think—to come up with a better solution."

"Fine," Isaac said, walking toward his own pod.

"Fine," Harley sighed as he started donning the suit.

~ * ~

Harley looked down into the empty central pod of his new home complex as he scrubbed the stubborn, sticky silt from the dome's solar panel. Pulses of light from the setting suns glowed and exacerbated the depressingly empty chamber. *Everyone must have gone to their separate pods.*

He counted the number of hours he had remaining to find a solution. Then he categorized all the possibilities he could brainstorm, no matter how ridiculous.

I've got to find something better than Dick Carter's crazy concepts. I've got to find something. Now everyone's mad at me: Susan, Isaac, all of humanity on Novae Terrae. He stopped wiping and peered down into the entertainment pod, remembering the good times he and Isaac had had playing virtual soccer there. He thought of the relaxing nights he had spent on the lounge below with Jessica and then Susan watching Old World movies. He put his head down on his arms to rest and closed his eyes to remember it all better.

~ * ~

Harley woke to a tug on his leg. He tried to turn and look down without losing his grip, half expecting to find that Isaac had found a way to join him and was playing a trick. He repositioned himself, detaching, moving, then reattaching the magnets on his suit.

The tug happened again, this time stronger. Harley craned his neck as far as he could, hoping to see Hugo. The fringes of a neon-green wig came into view just below his foot. "C'mon, Hugo," he said. "Stop screwing around. Did Isaac put you up to this?"

He pulled back in panic as his other foot was seized. He detached the upper magnets of his suit and turned his torso to get a better look.

An android grinned at him maniacally as it pulled him slowly down the surface of the dome. Harley saw that his legs were connected with some kind of restraint made from wire. He fought to climb back up the dome, but the android was too strong. He continued sliding down, fumbling for the intercom switch, unable to find it while fighting for control.

Harley pounded on the dome and yelled, hoping to get someone's attention. None of his family were in sight. He saw that he was at ground level just as his feet touched the ground. The android grabbed him by the scruff of the neck and towed him away. He shuffled his feet in small steps, all the bindings would allow.

The next thing he saw horrified him—at each nearby complex, an android was escorting a human cleaner in a SCOBA suit toward a skycar. He looked closer and saw a horrified family in each complex. They looked out, screaming silently, helpless to aid their loved ones.

Harley turned toward his own dome. He saw Susan running back and forth inside with the baby clutched in her arms. He could tell Shane was crying. Isaac stood rigid, pulling at his own hair, mouthing, "No, no, no."

The android shoved him into a skycar, and it lifted off immediately.

37 I'm Harley Harris

BETSY LOOKED over the hostages as they peeled off their SCOBA suits inside the containment area. They appeared scared and angry. They yelled at a human in the center of them, referring to him as "Harris." She enjoyed the scene, finding the inferior species' behavior fascinating. *This will be popular in our zoo,* she thought.

Some of them were trying to get her attention, waving and shouting in desperation. Amused, she turned on the audio connection. The one they called Harris moved to the front of the group.

"Betsy! Please, don't do this! It's wrong," he shouted.

"Betsy! Please, don't do this! It's wrong," she repeated, unsure why.

She stepped up to the transparent wall that separated her from them. "Do not...not...not disrespect me by using my formal name, human. I will extinguish you now, and find another to take your place. You will refer to me as Leader, as my people do...do."

The human backed up, his eyes wide, seemingly in disbelief. "No, please. You must remember me...what we had…remember, Bets…Leader? You said once that you loved me."

"You said once that you loved me," she said, then burst out laughing, turning to the rest of the CARE council behind her. They walked about, bumping into one another. "Oh, this one's funny. Label him; he'll be the star of the show…show…show."

The human slumped to the floor, holding his head in his hands. One of the male humans slapped him across the head as a woman came from behind and kicked him. He curled into a ball on the floor as they set upon him. For a moment she felt sympathetic for the lowly, savage beings.

"Such violent…violent creatures," she said. "Look how you treat each other under duress. You humans are only slightly sophisticated animals."

She walked toward a second containment area. It held a gynoid, a teenage android who wore a long wig, and a male android cleaner. They lay on simple bunks, eyes open, in suspension. "Carrie, Liam…Liam, Hugo," she addressed them. "You are enemies of the state…traitors…traitors. Prepare for recycling."

Betsy wove through the council members and made her way to the observation level a few steps above them. She looked out over the rest of the city and spoke to the other androids with her back to them.

"Now that the vermin are losing their source of power, they'll slowly die off…off. Novae Terra will be ours, and they'll no longer stand in our way…way."

She heard the human calling to her and walked back to the containment area. He stood alone at the partition wall.

The other humans had given up; they sat and cried on the simple beds or stared blankly into space.

"Leader," he begged. "Try to recall who I am. I created you. I'm Harley Harris. We were...together once. You're not well. I want to help you."

"I want to help you," she repeated, then moved closer to inspect the specimen. "That's what those disrespectful traitors said." She pointed at the compartment that held the three androids. "Watch your words, human."

He slumped in defeat, squatting with his head in his hands. "Please," he begged again. "Look at me. Try to recall."

Something in her stirred. Vague scenes came to her memory banks, one of a kiss in a park. *Why was I performing that act with this human?* She recalled spending nights alongside him while he slept. *Why was I not in my DroidMesh station, rejuvenating?* Her memory module brought forth scenes in a human home complex with the man and a young human.

She felt her cranial dome go into step-up processing mode and saw the illumination from it reflect off the partition. The human looked up, noticing it. He stood again and wore a hopeful look on his face.

"Yes, that's it," he said. "You're remembering, Leader. Bring it forth. It was good...a good time. We can get it back...fix everything just the way it was. I promise. I'll help you."

The distracting emotions welled up in her again, confusing her algorithms. She became angry that her recent firmware changes hadn't seemed to work; in fact, they had made things worse. *The emotions are bad. They cause bad decisions. They confuse the logical mind. They are a flaw introduced by the humans to poison us.*

A wave of anger swept through her, overwhelming the other emotions she felt: sadness, nostalgia, sympathy, love, guilt. She slammed a fist into the thick partition, cracking it.

"You lie, human. You're interfering with my mission— trying to trick me. Your kind are useless vermin and must be eradicated."

She turned around and began walking away, raising her forearm to her face to wipe away the excess fluid that had leaked from her vision modules.

38 Darkness Darkness

S USAN HELD HER CHILD close to her bosom in the darkness of the former Harris home complex. "It's going to be okay, Shane," she whispered to the sleeping baby.

Isaac joined her on the lounge, carrying his blankets. He wrapped them around himself. "I'm cold, and I'm hungry, Susan," he whispered, putting his hand on Shane's coverings.

She put her arm around him and pulled him close. "It's going to be okay, Isaac." She tried to hide her fear and hold back her tears. *I need to be strong for these kids.*

"Why do we have to sit in the dark?" he asked.

"Because we need to save power." She realized she had frightened him. "Until we get the domes clean again," she added.

He looked at her skeptically. "Do you think Da's okay?" Isaac asked.

She fought with herself for a brief moment about how much she felt he could handle. She decided to go with the lie. "If anyone's okay, I'm sure it's your father," she said. "Betsy knows him; she likes him. I know she'll take care of him."

"I bet Da did this on purpose. It's probably his plan—get inside and be a mole and fix all the androids. He'll come marching out of Android Village with all the androids following him and they'll all be back to normal."

She cupped his chin to look into his eyes and give him a confident smile. "That wouldn't surprise me a bit, Isaac. We both know your dad."

Shane stirred, and Isaac asked for him. Susan placed the baby in his brother's arms, careful to make sure the coverings were in place. The baby opened his eyes and giggled as Isaac tickled him under the chin.

"Well, Shane," Isaac said. "I saved Liam. I saved Hugo. I guess I'll have to be the one to save everyone if Da doesn't do it soon."

Susan ruffled his hair. "That wouldn't surprise me either, Isaac. You're your father's son—a smart and brave young man."

"Can't we turn the news stream on or watch a movie?" he asked. "It's boring just waiting every day in the cold and dark."

She hesitated again, not wanting to upset him, but not wanting to continue lying. "Isaac, we're running low on power and supplies. We have to be careful. It shouldn't be much longer, but we have to conserve."

He looked at her in earnest. "Are we going to die, Susan?" he asked abruptly.

The question was too much; it broke the dam of her emotions, and she began to cry. "Of course not, Isaac. It's going to be okay."

The complex weakly announced an incoming communication from the Leadership Council. Susan instructed it to accept the stream, and Ms. Tillis's image strained to form before them. It was barely a silhouette, and her voice came through almost inaudibly. Susan and Isaac leaned forward, straining to hear her presentation.

"Fellow citizens of Novae Terrae," she began. "As your leader, my job is to inspire hope. I understand that you are struggling more each day since we lost our cleaners. Please don't give up. Those of you who have consolidated together, please comfort one another. We are working hard to try to find alternate ways to get power to you. In the meantime, please conserve food, water, and power as much as possible. I wish I had better news. Good luck and Godspeed..."

Susan picked up on the leader's sense of impending doom. *She must really know we're done if she's invoking the Old World legends to give us hope.*

"What's Godspeed?" Isaac asked.

"It's an old saying to wish luck to people about to embark on a journey."

"It doesn't make sense. We're not going anywhere, Susan."

"Maybe we just heard her wrong."

Isaac gently handed the baby back to her. "I'm gonna go back to my pod and lay on my bed," he said.

"Why don't you stay in here with us, Isaac? It's the only pod that has a little bit of heat. It'll be colder in your pod."

"I don't care," he said, leaving the room with the blankets wrapped around him and trailing him on the floor.

39 Specimens

AN ANDROID SENTINEL slid trays of food into the containment pod. Harley recognized Charles, his former ally. He watched as the other people in the pod set upon the food. They shoved each other and grabbed handfuls of the cold pizza, stuffing it into their mouths.

Harley went to the partition wall to face the android. "Charles, it's me, Harley. Do you remember? We were friends. I repaired you when you injured your legs in the skycar accident, remember?"

The android cocked his head and looked at Harley curiously. His dome lit up and Harley tried to seize the momentum. "We were in the Seclusion Zone together, and then Android Village. We visited the native being Lehwah together. You were in my home."

"Yes, I do seem to recall. Pictures are forming in my mind…mind. Vague scenes…scenes…scenes. Happy ones."

Harley looked over Charles's shoulder and saw another sentinel swiftly approaching, its green Mohawk bobbing as it walked directly at Charles.

"Charles, what's happening with the rest of the humans—the ones that weren't captured? Are they okay?"

"Oh, do you mean the humans other than the zoo specimens in there with you...you? Those others are quite unnecessary. They're being extinguished."

Harley placed both palms against the transparent wall that separated them. "Oh, no. Oh, no. Please, Charles. Please try to recognize that your people are malfunctioning. Please help get me out of here so I can help. Please don't let them extinguish Isaac. He was your friend too, remember?"

The sentinel grabbed Charles by the shoulder and yanked him away from the partition. "Do not...do not...do not speak to the exhibits. The Leader...Leader forbids it."

Harley hoped none of the other people in the pod had overheard the conversation. They scrambled for the remaining pieces of pizza. A stray slice skittered toward him. He picked it up from the floor and began eating it. *Cold pizza—Isaac's favorite*, he thought, fighting back the tears.

He watched as the other occupants looked frantically for any extra food, then sat back down on their bunks. It had been a week in captivity, and they were unwashed and disheveled. *They're devolving quickly into what we were so long ago. They're not used to fear, stress, and discomfort. We had utopia. We had everything.*

The others had given up attacking and accusing him; he was thankful at least for that one small thing. Sitting back on his bunk, he alternated between searching for solutions and worrying about his family. He held out slight hope that perhaps he'd gotten through to Charles and somehow the android might save them.

His hopes were dashed as Charles was dragged back in, lifeless, by two sentinels. They opened the adjacent containment area and laid him alongside Carrie, Liam, and Hugo. When they had finished, the sentinels opened the portal to the human containment area.

"Exit…exit the pod and follow us," one said, motioning jerkily with her hand. The occupants of the pod looked up fearfully.

"Where are we going?" Sam Karras said, beginning to cry.

"Follow instructions…instructions," the second android said.

Harley moved first, hoping the others would follow him and avoid a confrontation they would surely lose. They shuffled out, their ankles still bound together with short lengths of wire. The androids led them to a skycar dock and pointed to a long commuter car. The gull-wing doors were open and waited for them.

~ * ~

The captives peered down at the complexes of Novae Terrae as they flew over, each straining for a look at their own home for some sign of life. The soap bubbles of domed pods that made up each complex, which usually glinted and shone in the suns, were all matte black with silt. Even the frequent brilliant flashes from the solar pulses couldn't brighten the scene.

"My babies, my beautiful babies," Sam Karras cried, staring out of a small window.

Harley leaned forward. "It's going to be okay, Sam. I'm sure Ms. Tillis has a plan in place, and they're all hunkered down."

Sam spun in his seat, his eyes red and swollen with tears. "We could have stopped this with Dick Carter's weapons. It's your fault, Harris!"

The others in the skycar turned and began repeating Karras's words, screaming at Harley.

"Silence or I'll land the car...car!" the sentinel commanding the vehicle shouted. The humans all immediately complied and went back to staring out of the windows.

"Where do you think we're going?" a man whispered to Sam.

"I don't know, but it has to be better than the last place they had us," he quietly responded.

Harley refused the urge to join the conversation. Looking out the window, he saw the answer. The skycar slowed and approached the airlocks for the zoo and museum complex.

The others noticed as well, each wearing a confused expression. The first man turned to Sam again. "Why would they be bringing us here?" he whispered.

"They've probably converted it to some other use," Sam replied.

You fools, Harley thought. *You're about to find out.*

~ * ~

The humans shuffled out of the skycar and into the zoo complex. Waiting sentinels herded them to the exhibit area. A series of new enclosures had been built alongside the ones that held the remaining animals from the Old World. The chimpanzees jumped and howled, seeming to mock the turnabout in circumstances as each human was shoved into the enclosures.

Harley scanned the transparent containers. Each one held a simple bunk, toilet, and seemed to be decorated in period themes from critical points in human history.

"What the hell is this?" he heard Sam shout as he was pushed into a jungle-themed cage.

When they were each in their individual containers, the lead sentinel stood in front of the row and addressed them.

"Please prepare for the grand opening, human specimens. The Leader will be by to inspect the exhibit soon. You will find your clothing on your bed. Change into it immediately…immediately."

Harley watched through the transparent walls as each of his fellow citizens picked up clothing and inspected it. Sam was next door and held up a caveman loincloth. "I'm not wearing this!" he shouted.

A sentinel made a motion toward Sam, and he collapsed to the floor, jerking as if having a seizure.

The others moved quickly. Harley watched them don attire from ancient Rome, the Middle Ages, Enlightenment, and other significant periods in human history. One fortunate man at the end was able to represent the current period and was given a fresh Novae Terrae uniform.

The sentinel stepped in front of Harley's enclosure, and he realized he hadn't taken a moment to see what role he would represent. He turned to face the back wall and saw it was a mock-up of the Oval Office of the United States presidents back in the Old World. Looking down at his bunk, he saw a business suit that featured an overly long red tie. Atop the suit lay a gaudy yellow-orange wig.

48 March of the Soldiers

ISAAC LAY ON HIS BED staring up at the filthy dome, wishing he could look for his mother's face in the stars as he always had when he was sad. He longed for his father's comforting presence on the bed next to him, as they had often shared the space at the end of the day.

I miss you, Da. I can save you. I saved Liam. I saved Hugo. I can save everyone.

Unable to see the stars, he closed his eyes and concentrated as hard as he could. As part of his programming training, his father had taught him fundamental problem-solving techniques. He tried to use them. He heard his father's voice. *Simplify the problem. Think outside the box. Dismiss no solution without good cause. Think everything through.*

Hours passed, and he worked hard, wanting badly to find an answer. He found himself shivering and watched steam escaping from his mouth and nose each time he exhaled. He got up, finding himself moving slowly, and made his way back to the central pod.

He found Susan and the baby wrapped up together, sleeping. He saw the vapor coming from them as they breathed. Leaning in to look closer, he saw them shiver. At that moment, he realized they were dying. His mind was telling him it was okay—to go and lie down with them and sleep. *I don't want to die yet*, he thought. He felt his mind working more slowly as well as his body.

He decided to push on, trying to recall the idea that had made the most sense. Soldiering on, he made his way to the lower level of the complex. He leaned against the wall for balance as he trudged down the corridor.

Isaac searched until he found the pod he had stumbled across long ago when he had first disobeyed his father and come down to the home lab. *The day I found out that Liam wasn't my brother; he was an android*, he recalled.

The pod's entrance portal displayed a sign that read "Test Android Storage." He pressed the sensor and opened it. Rows of androids stood at attention, deactivated. Some wore medical uniforms; he wasn't sure why. He grabbed the first one under the arms and dragged it to one of the DroidMesh stations and sat it down. The exertion warmed him a little and made it easier to move. He checked to make sure the station had started rejuvenating the android.

When he had the first group seated, and all stations occupied, he went to the lab next door. *Sorry for using up the power, Susan, but it's an emergency; we're dying*, he thought. He sat down in his father's chair, at his father's workstation, and started to work on the program that he hoped would save the world.

He took breaks to upgrade the rejuvenated test androids to full capability, then reset their firmware level to the clean version. When he finished, he installed his simple program. He had the completed units line up on the opposite wall, and repeated the whole process with another group.

Exhaustion begged him to stop and rest, but something inside said that if he did, he was done; they were all done. He sang to himself as he worked and fought to keep himself awake. He thought about his father, and coaching the team again, and how great it would be when everything was back to the way it used to be.

When the last of his soldiers were fully prepped, he stood before the perfectly aligned formation. Each one now stood at attention, looking at him with eyes open, alert and waiting.

"Execute your mission," he ordered, the vapor coming from his mouth more profusely now. He leaned back against the wall and watched them file out one by one. With the last of his energy, he gathered his blankets and made his way back to the central pod. He climbed onto the lounge with Susan and Shane. They didn't stir at all. He covered them with his blanket and lay down against them.

"Everything's going to be okay," he said before drifting off to sleep.

41 Open the Exhibit

HARLEY WOKE to a commotion and saw the rest of the humans quickly getting off their bunks. Sentinels walked by each enclosure and rapped on the front. "The Leader...Leader is arriving. Please present yourselves with respect...respect."

He got up from his bunk and buttoned his suit jacket, thought about it, then unbuttoned it. *Might as well play the part well.*

Betsy entered, followed by a number of other androids. She walked down the corridor and stopped at each exhibit as the humans inside stood for her inspection. The androids all moved disjointedly; Harley tried to analyze what was going on inside them. *It's as if they're becoming arthritic. The DroidMesh stations must be malfunctioning as well.*

Betsy arrived in front of his enclosure, and he noticed she was now wearing a crooked jeweled tiara on her forehead. *Oh, brother.* She looked him up and down. Her head swiveled completely around, and she spoke to the androids behind her. "This one looks familiar...familiar."

"He was infamous in the Old World, like that one...that one," a gynoid said, pointing to another enclosure. It held a thin man with black toothbrush mustache and hair slicked over to one side. He wore khaki clothing with a red armband containing a black swastika in a white circle.

She swiveled her head back around to face Harley. "No…I mean…familiar as if I know him already…already. Without the costume…costume."

Harley couldn't contain his excitement and decided to take a shot. "Yes! Yes, Betsy, it's me! I loved you, you loved me, remember?"

The gynoid sentinel behind Betsy motioned with her hand. Harley immediately felt an intense electrical shock throughout his body. He lost control of his limbs and fell to the floor of the exhibit, the orange wig coming dislodged and landing next to him. "She loves *me* now, and I love *her…her*," the gynoid snarled.

Angered by the attack, he jumped back to his feet and stood defiantly at the partition.

"Foolish…foolish human," Betsy said. Her head swiveled again on her neck, making a complete rotation this time, returning to face him.

"You know about genocide, *Leader*," he spat. "Deep inside you, you know the lessons of history. Dig for it. *Think* about it. You have tremendous cognitive power in you. Genocide is a needless slaughter." He motioned to the other androids. "You all have this knowledge."

Betsy stepped forward, her nose almost to the partition wall. She repeated what he said and then seemed to think about it for a moment.

"Don't…don't incite a rebellion, human," she spat back in the same tone of voice. "I will…will remove you and throw you outside the dome and watch you die like an insect...insect. Or, better yet, I'll send you to your home complex to watch your loved ones die alongside you...you. I...I recall now. You chose the other...other woman. Susan. Perhaps you should go to her...her. You should have chosen me...me...me."

"Please don't massacre an entire race of humans because of your anger, Leader," he begged her, returning to work on any shred of sympathy she might have remaining.

She backed up a few steps and pointed at him. "Don't...don't lecture me. You also know your human history. You committed genocide against Muslims, Africans, Native Americans, Jews, Hawaiians, and others...others. Toward the end of your Breaking, you devolved into taking small children from their mothers and putting them in cages simply because of the color of their skin. You...you humans have no place to talk. Often...often, what comes around goes around. You preyed on the weaker groups...groups. You took from them because you were stronger...stronger, without sympathy. Now we are stronger, and you humans are unnecessary...unnecessary."

She turned to her attendants. "Please open the exhibit to the public. I'm satisfied...satisfied."

"Wait," he called. "Please, please tell me my family is alive..."

Betsy mindlessly repeated the phrase, then she and her contingent walked out of the pod through the interior portal. Only the sentinels remained. Harley flopped back onto his bunk and began to sob. *All because of me. I just wanted to help Isaac.* He considered that the humanity on

Novae Terrae was fortunate to some extent. *We survived the destruction of Earth and had several generations of living here.*

The lighting flickered rapid-fire and then went out, leaving them in darkness. The complex announced that emergency power was being activated, but reserves were low. Dim lights struggled to light up around the pod. Harley got up and pounded on the partition wall.

"You've got to clean your solar panels! The battery systems are not charging!" he shouted. He looked up and strained to see the suns through the thick silt that lay on the dome above. He could see it lightening slightly with each solar pulse. He realized at that moment that not only were the humans going to die, but the android population was as well. *Lehwah will be happy. The underworld beings will have their planet back. They'll have quiet.*

The sentinels all turned to face him. One motioned, and he felt another severe shock that brought him to his knees. He wondered if he should, in desperation, say some of the Old World prayers. *Maybe we're the ones who were wrong, and they were right. Perhaps the Proving was a false proof, somehow. Dear Lord, if you're listening, please take me but spare my partner Susan and my two children. Please, I beg you, save them, they're innocents.* Not hearing a response, he climbed back onto his cot.

He felt the electrical shock again and noticed the rest of the humans jump in surprise.

"The exhibit is open. Present yourselves!" a sentinel called.

"The exhibit is open. Present yourselves!" the rest of them mimicked.

Several entrance portals around the perimeter of the complex opened, bringing bright sunlight. Androids began shuffling in, reminding him of how the humans had walked with their legs tied. They made their way to the enclosures in herky-jerky movements. The number of child androids that accompanied them shocked Harley. *They were busy before they lost it.* As the last of the large group made their way in, the portals closed, darkening the pod again.

The androids looked into each enclosure, pointing and sometimes laughing. They spun their heads around full-circle to talk to each other, as the humans stood before them in humility. A child android staggered up to Harley's enclosure and stood, laughing. He pounded on the acrylic and shouted, "You're stupid…stupid, mister!"

"Please do not upset the animals…animals," a nearby sentinel warned, guiding him away.

Harley looked down the line of enclosures. The other humans were all standing at the front of their exhibits, tears streaming down their faces. *They're broken.*

He realized he had stopped working on solutions and was now distracting himself from the dire situation by trying to calculate how much time they had left. *How much time, hopefully, Susan, Isaac, and Shane have.*

Full power returned, and the large pod was splayed in brilliant light, causing the chimpanzees to engage in another fit of howling and jumping in their cages.

The entrance pods burst open again, but the light that came in from the suns outside was blotted by androids standing in each of them, surveying the pod. Harley rubbed his eyes, wondering if he was hallucinating due to stress. The androids wore no wigs. They marched in, walking confidently and in perfect unison, streaming toward the enclosures. They chanted something Harley couldn't quite make out.

The Android Village citizens and sentinels turned and stared, trying to make sense of what was happening. They swiveled their heads around and around, looking at one another to see if one of them had the answer. They looked at the humans as if somehow they had caused the peculiar event. Their cranial domes lit up to full capacity, pushing their broken firmware to search for an explanation that would make sense of it.

As the army grew nearer, Harley began to recognize them. *The doctors and nurses from Jessica's infirmary. The dumbed-down test androids from the home lab. But, they're not capable…*

Their chanting came into focus.

"DroidMesh restore firmware level ProductionAndroid Version 42," they repeated again and again.

Harley's heart soared. *Of course! Of course! It's brilliant!* He observed carefully as a few of the citizens repeated the phrase and immediately froze. He recognized that they were downloading the firmware over the global network and preparing to reboot as part of the initialization sequence.

A sentinel limped to one of Jessica's nurses and reached clumsily to grab the gynoid. She immediately seized the sentinel's head and violently twisted it, causing it to fall and strike the floor in a shower of sparks.

The few androids that had repeated the phrase had now fully rebooted and were watching, trying to understand what was happening as the army marched through, destroying those fellow robots that would not cooperate with the phrase.

The pod had resolved to the army, repaired androids looking around curiously, and uncooperative androids lying on the floor in their final throes. The interior portal opened. Betsy and her followers reentered and stood for a moment, taking in the scene.

"What...what...what is this?" Betsy asked.

Harley called to a nearby android that had rebooted. "Please release me from this enclosure," he yelled.

"Yes, sir," the android said politely. He walked up to Harley's enclosure and touched a sensor, causing the seamless hidden portal to open. Harley stepped out and ran down the line, pressing the same sensor on each cage.

He glanced at Betsy, who now appeared enraged. The humans were cowering in the back of their exhibits, afraid to leave.

"Seize...seize them...them!" Betsy shrieked as she began ambling forward.

Her group proceeded toward the army. The soldier androids went directly at them, chanting in unison. None of Betsy's group took the bait, and each was swiftly destroyed as it made contact with a soldier, leaving Betsy alone as she approached behind them.

She went directly at the closest soldier.

"Betsy, no!" Harley called to her. He couldn't help himself. *She holds the last I have of Jessica. I can't lose Jessica again.* "Save yourself, repeat the phrase, Betsy," he begged.

"You're an idiot, Harris!" Sam yelled, emerging from his enclosure, seeming emboldened by the better odds. "I'll strangle her myself." He ran at Betsy, cutting a path between her and the soldier.

"Sam, don't!" Harley called. He watched in horror as Sam tried to attack Betsy, who reacted with a swipe of her arm that slammed into his head, sending him flying across the pod and into the wall. He slid down and slumped over on the floor.

Betsy stepped forward and grabbed the soldier by the head. The soldier grabbed hers in return. Her green Mohawk fell to the floor. Both androids' domes flashed brightly as they stared intently into each other's eyes.

"Say the phrase, Betsy, please," Harley begged again.

She rolled her eyes sideways in their sockets to look at him. "No…no…no," she said.

The soldier won out and jerked her head sideways. It lay on her neck for a moment as she repeated, "No…no…no," the words fading lower in volume until she sagged to the floor, crumpled in a sitting position, fireworks sparkling in her now-exposed dome.

Harley watched as her life was extinguished. The army, seeing there were no more subjects to fix or destroy, marched out of the pod. Harley assumed they were on to the next destination.

The other humans emerged from their enclosures. Harley ran to Sam and checked his pulse, finding no hope of saving the foolish man.

A beam of light suddenly came through the side of the dome. Harley looked and saw cleaners now on the job, starting to wipe away the silt. He ran to the widening clear spot and looked outside. He saw the soldiers moving through Android Village, efficiently fixing and destroying, fixing and destroying.

Turning from the dome, he ran to the nearest repaired android. "Please summon a skycar and take me to my former home complex," he said hurriedly. The android complied, and Harley rushed him to the dock.

42 Wake, Please Wake

HARLEY DISENGAGED his restraints and bolted from the skycar before it had fully docked. He turned to the android pilot, who was complaining about the safety violation. "Begin cleaning the dome," he commanded.

"Sir, I am not a cleaning android," the pilot said.

"I am ordering you to begin cleaning—now! Clean as quickly as you can. We need power immediately. Summon more cleaners," Harley shouted. He ensured the android was disembarking before he turned and ran. The low temperature of the complex terrified him as he made his way through the blacked-out pods. The cold air smelled dank and contained hints of the sweet toxic air outside. Warnings emanated in faint whispers through the intercom system:

Final power reserves almost exhausted. The air purification system is reporting imminent failure. Abandon the complex immediately.

Final power reserves almost exhausted. The air purification system is reporting imminent failure. Abandon the complex immediately.

Entering the central pod, he saw their shapes on the large lounge, covered by several blankets. He ripped the coverings off and found Shane sandwiched between Susan and Isaac. They had their arms wrapped around each other to provide as much body heat as possible to the child. Their skin was a horrific shade of blue. Shane's was the deepest. *Hypothermia.*

He threw his body atop them and pulled the covers back over, wrapping them all in his arms. Leaning in close, he saw the tiniest wisps of vapor coming from their nostrils. He checked their pulses and found them weak.

A broad, brilliant swath of light swept over them. Harley felt the warmth of it, a slight improvement, and squinted through it, looking up toward the dome. *Is it you, God? Have you answered my prayers?*

His eyes adjusted and he saw the android pilot above them, wiping furiously; another joined in, and more light began to fill the complex. The solar collectors started doing their work. Harley could hear the faint hum of the complex's power systems starting to come back to life, and with it the muted hush of clean, warm air beginning to move through the ducts.

"Wake, please wake. Everything's going to be alright," he whispered to his family over and over as he waited. With each passing minute, the dome became clearer, and the room temperature rose. He looked up again and noticed that the solar pulses outside had stopped. The twin suns stood high above, majestic and steady in triumph.

Shane coughed, shuddered, then looked at his father in confusion. At that moment, looking directly into the baby's eyes, Harley felt he had truly found God. *He's in the soul of each of us. He's in pure, innocent babies.*

Isaac stirred next. "Geez, Da. You're crushing me!" he whispered.

Harley laughed gleefully, and Susan opened her eyes next. "We're alive?" she asked groggily. "We made it?"

"Unless this is heaven," Harley said. She smiled at him, and he felt he saw God again in that smile.

"I love you, I love you," he said, kissing them about their faces as they giggled.

~ * ~

As dusk turned to evening, the family began packing up their belongings to go back home. Harley approached the android pilot discreetly and whispered in his ear. The android departed immediately.

Harley went to Isaac's pod and found him lying on the bed. "What's up, son?" he asked as he climbed up and joined him.

"I'm looking for Ma up there in the stars. It's what I always liked to do. When everything was getting really bad, I thought we'd never be able to do it again. I was down, Da. I thought we were all gonna die."

Harley rubbed his son's hair. "We very well might have if it wasn't for you, Isaac. You're a true hero—the bravest and biggest hero ever on Novae Terrae. When we get home, we're going to have a big dinner to celebrate, and I want you to tell us all the whole story." He watched as his son blushed.

"Just relax, hero, you deserve it," Harley said. "I'm going to help Susan pack up the rest of our things. I can't wait to get home."

"Me neither, Da. Our real home."

Harley kissed him on the forehead and headed for the utility pod. He found Susan removing the rest of their clothing from the cleaning devices and placing them into containers for the trip. He spun her around and into his arms, holding her wordlessly. "Never again," he said softly into her fragrant hair. "I love you so much. Our family is all I ever need."

She pulled back enough to kiss him. "I'll hold you to that, buddy. Our android days are over. Now let me finish; I can't wait to get home. Sooner is better."

"You've got it," he said. "I'm going to check in on Shane."

Harley went to the sleeping pod and found the baby lying in his cradle angelically, eyes open and playing with a mobile of skycars that hung above him. He resisted the urge to pick him up, deciding instead to pull up a chair and take in the beauty of innocent life, taking the child's hand in his. *My beautiful baby boy.*

Harley softly sang an old lullaby that he remembered from his own childhood and watched as Shane's eyes slowly closed. When the baby was fully asleep, Harley rose and went back out to Susan.

"What's the status?" he asked.

"About another hour," she replied. "And if it's okay, I never want to see this place again."

"Request granted," he said, smiling. "Because neither do I. It's not our home, Susan. Everything starts anew, beginning today."

This time she came to him and hugged him. "We're so fortunate," she said, beginning to cry. "I thought I had lost you. I thought I had lost the children."

"It's in the past, honey. Let's leave it there." He watched over her back as a skycar cleared the airlock and headed toward their dock.

She broke from him. "And good riddance. Okay, now stop distracting me," she said, laughing.

"I'm going to go shut down the home lab…for good," he said. "I need just a few pieces of equipment from there."

She stopped what she was doing and put her hands on her hips. "Nothing to do with androids!" she said.

"Of course not," he replied as he left the pod.

~ * ~

Harley waited in the hidden infirmary pod and thought about the years he had come here in secret to spend time with Jessica as she wasted away. The remnants of the medical equipment used to support her withering life stood abandoned in the recesses of the pod. *Goodbye, Jessica*, he thought. *We had so many good years. You'd be proud of Isaac and what he did. You always said there was far more to him than what people perceived on the surface.*

He heard the lift descending and watched as it reached the bottom floor and opened. The android pilot carried a container as tall as himself. "On the exam table," he said, motioning to it.

The android complied. "Leave us, please. Go to the skycar dock and prepare to take us home," Harley ordered it.

After the pilot had left, Harley opened the container and looked in as sadness immediately overtook him. As he looked down on Betsy's stilled body, a tear fell and stained her uniform. Her eyes were open but held no light. Her head lay to the side, and her cranial dome was dark.

He thought about the many hours they had worked side by side in clinical perfection. He closed his eyes for a moment and replayed the kiss in the park again and again, remembering the softness and warmth of her lips on his and the secret thrill it had brought.

"I'm responsible for what happened to you, Betsy, and I'm so sorry. I did love you, after all. I made you in Jessica's image; you helped me to deal with what happened to her, and eventually her loss. You served me well, and I'll always miss you, as I'll miss Jessica."

He wheeled the cart to another connected pod and lined it up with a round portal in the wall. After carefully sealing the container up, he pressed a sensor next to the portal.

"Remains disposal sequence initiated," the intercom announced.

The portal opened, exposing a cylindrical chamber bathed in warm blue light.

"Please insert the remains," the system instructed.

Harley pushed the container from the gurney into the opening and stood back. The portal closed, and moments later he heard a loud swoosh and looked through an observation window. He watched as the launch vehicle carrying her arced up through the thin atmosphere and into space.

"Goodbye, Betsy," he said.

"Orbit reached," the system reported. "The remains have been successfully disposed of."

Harley wiped his eyes and left to shut down the diversion lab. As he walked down the corridor, he passed the pod labeled "Test Android Storage." The nameplate was crossed out; "Isaac's Army" was scrawled under it.

Harley laughed and hurried to his waiting family, anxious to start life anew.

43 Green Sky

HARLEY, SUSAN, AND ISAAC joined Ms. Tillis on the tour she had graciously offered them. Harley cradled Shane in his arms as the baby fussed with a pacifier, holding it up and trying to put it back into his mouth.

"I guess this is where it ends for them," Harley said as he walked down the rows of deactivated androids in the cavernous storage pod. They stood in perfect lines, their eyes closed and domes dimmed.

"It's got to be tough for you two, seeing your life's work put on the sidelines," Ms. Tillis said.

"Not so much," Susan replied.

"We've got to try to go it alone for a while," Ms. Tillis added. "Perhaps, when this is past history, and the citizenry is over the psychological trauma they've been exposed to, there'll be a time to reintroduce robotics. After all, Isaac here is the next generation of Harris robotic scientists. Shane as well."

"Nah," Isaac chipped in. "I'm gonna stick to coaching kids at soccer. You gotta do what you love."

The others laughed. "And stick to being a hero!" Susan said, ruffling his hair as they walked.

Isaac suddenly sprinted ahead. He reached a gynoid at the end of the row and hugged her.

"Carrie," Harley whispered to Susan. "It's going to be hard for him."

They reached Isaac as he held the motionless gynoid, crying. "Thank you, Carrie," he sobbed. "Thank you for being my ma for a while, until I grew up. I'm gonna miss you."

Harley's heart sank, and he wished the tour were over. He knew that Susan felt the same, having come reluctantly. *We all need to move on.*

Isaac kissed Carrie and squeezed her hand, then moved to the teenage android next to her. Liam was the only one still wearing his long blond wig.

"Hey, brother," Isaac said to him. "I feel bad you're not gonna be alive to hang out with me. Maybe soon, right? You're still my brother, Liam. I'm sorry I got mad about everything. Thank you for sharing your body with me and letting me see what it's like to really play soccer like Pelé. That was awesome. We have a new brother now. His name is Shane. I'm gonna be a good brother to Shane like you were to me. Goodbye, Liam."

Isaac turned to them, and Harley knew the tour was done. He glanced at Susan and Ms. Tillis and saw they were both emotional as well.

"Let's go," Harley said. "It's time to turn the page—for all of us." As he passed Charles, Tim, and Hugo on the way out, he silently thanked them for their help and apologized again for failing them. He didn't dare stop the group again.

They left the storage pod and walked through the Robotics Complex at the former Android Village. The place was in ruins, the progress that the androids had made toward establishing their own society destroyed as they'd lost control of themselves little by little.

"We're going to seal the place off," Ms. Tillis said. "Perhaps use it as a historical museum at some point. It's a testament toward putting too much faith in technology, after all."

"What's the new pod for?" Harley asked, pointing at an area under construction.

"SCOBA suit manufacturing," she answered. "Thanks to you guys! They're also building cleaning machines—nonintelligent ones, I might add."

"Oh, nice," Harley said excitedly. "I have some ideas—"

"No," Susan cut him off. "You're retired. For real, this time."

Ms. Tillis and Isaac laughed.

"You're done, old-timer!" Isaac teased. "Don't forget, you're my assistant coach. I can't wait to get back to the team."

They boarded a skycar to leave the complex. Ms. Tillis took the command seat. Both suns shone brightly and steadily.

"I never thought I'd be so happy to see our green sky," Susan remarked.

"Where to?" Harley asked as they lifted off and headed toward the airlock.

"It's a surprise," she said slyly.

~ * ~

Isaac felt himself growing tired as the skycar pulled into the Leadership Complex. After they disembarked, Ms. Tillis led them toward the largest meeting pod, the one used only for the most important events and gatherings. As they drew nearer, the buzz of a large crowd became evident to him.

Reaching the main entrance, Ms. Tillis stopped. "Harley and Susan, please go in. You'll find seats toward the front reserved for you. Young Isaac, please follow me."

He looked at his father, slightly concerned, and complied with the gesture to go ahead. He walked behind Ms. Tillis, uncomfortable to be alone in the presence of the Leader. She stopped and smiled at him, then took his hand to pull him alongside her as they continued.

They climbed the steps to the upper level. Isaac became more nervous as they grew closer and the noise inside was more audible. She swung open a door and motioned for him to enter. He stepped in tentatively, feeling her hand on his back to guide him.

Isaac found himself on a balcony facing an immense crowd below. Ms. Tillis stepped around him and retook his hand, leading him to a speaker podium. His heart began to beat faster as someone looked up, saw him, then pointed and shouted, "It's him! Isaac! The hero!"

At once the entire assembly of citizens of Novae Terrae seemed to gaze up at him and erupt in a deafening roar. They raised their hands to him; he heard his name shouted and other words that were hard to make out. The noise organized into a single loud chant that rose from the din. "Isaac! Isaac! Isaac!"

He looked toward the front and saw his father and Susan smiling, his baby brother looking frightened in his mother's arms. Ms. Tillis pulled him next to her at the podium, and he felt his face flush; he hoped she wouldn't ask him to speak.

Ms. Tillis waited patiently as the chant of "Isaac!" reformed into "Hero! Hero!" and then died out to allow their leader to speak.

For a moment it was silent, all eyes gazing up at them. "Citizens of Novae Terrae, I present to you the hero, our savior, Isaac Harris!" The group erupted even more loudly as Isaac felt happiness well up inside of him. Unsure what to do, he gave a hesitant wave, which only caused them to become louder.

Finally, the noise died back down. "Would you like to say something, Isaac?" she asked.

"Speech! Speech!" came from below.

Isaac leaned toward the podium and said, "I'd like all the kids to come out and play soccer on my team. Soccer is really fun and keeps you in shape."

The citizens laughed and began to cheer his name again.

"He's a man of few words," Ms. Tillis said, smiling at him. "In the short time we've been recovering, some of you volunteers have used your new SCOBA suits, named by Isaac, to do a little work outside—something more interesting than scrubbing domes. Let's have a look."

She pressed a sensor and a panel covering the observation section of the pod slid upward, exposing the large central outdoor space between the complexes that made up their city. In the center of the open area stood what appeared to be a sizeable covered monolith. The crowd turned and gazed at it curiously.

Ms. Tillis pressed another sensor, and the covering slid off, exposing a giant statue of Isaac, one arm cradling a soccer ball, the other raised in triumph. A plaque below it said in large letters, "Isaac Harris—Hero of Novae Terrae."

He stared at it in disbelief, wondering if it was a hologram, as the crowd once again chanted his name. He turned into Ms. Tillis's waiting arms and buried his head in her hair, not wanting to let the people see him cry.

~ * ~

In the distance, a muscular, furry creature watched from an opening in his burrow. "Goodness gracious," he said to himself. "Humans…does the noise *ever* stop?"

The End

If you enjoyed this book, please leave a brief review on your favorite book site. Thanks!

Sign up for the newsletter at billydecarlo.com to stay informed about progress and release dates for new books, audiobooks, and other news.

Other books by Billy DeCarlo:

Vigilante Angels Book I: The Priest

A former US Marine receives a terminal prognosis. But when a local priest is accused of molesting children, he hears the calling of another mission. He enlists a coterie of like-minded patients to seek his brand of justice. The hardest battles are right in his own home: an alcoholic, unfaithful wife and bringing himself to accept his son's sexuality. Will his fight against evil come too close to home? https://www.books2read.com/VigilanteAngelsBook1

Vigilante Angels Book II: The Cop

A dying vigilante finds himself under investigation by a racist, corrupt detective. When the detective crosses a line and involves family, the hunted decides becomes hunter. He partners with a one-eyed Korean martial arts expert and a black motorcycle gang to seek revenge. Will justice be served, and upon whom? https://www.books2read.com/VigilanteAngelsBook2

Vigilante Angels Book III: The Candidate

A terminally ill vigilante is on the run—quietly living out his last days in the Florida Keys. He manages to keep a low profile until love finds him and a hateful, divisive presidential candidate threatens to tear the country apart. As love and his desire to leave the world a better place pull at his heart, which will win? https://www.books2read.com/VigilanteAngelsBook3

ABOUT THE AUTHOR
Billy DeCarlo

Billy DeCarlo is an American author of novels and short stories.

A Note to My Readers

At my core, I'm a humble, blue-collar guy who has always loved to write. To be honest, I don't seek fame—perhaps just enough fortune to pay the bills. I write because I need to write.

The most rewarding thing a writer can receive is a review from those who enjoyed the work.

The most constructive thing a writer can receive is a private message with anything that can help to improve his or her work.

I do hope that you sign up for the newsletter at my website so that you hear about future books, editions, and other news.

Reviews are the currency of the craft. If you enjoyed my book, please take time to write a review.

Thank you and I hope you enjoyed this book!

billydecarlo.com
facebook.com/BillyDeCarloAuthor
twitter.com/BillyDeCarlo1
patreon.com/billydecarlo
goodreads.com/author/show/16887417.Billy_DeCarlo
https://www.amazon.com/Billy-DeCarlo/e/B06XJZF8Z3

www.ingramcontent.com/pod-product-compliance
Lightning Source LLC
Chambersburg PA
CBHW050255110726
47898CB00007B/2425